...erie Lady ... ...omance series and a st... ... ... *The Skeleton in the Closet* – all pu... ...d by Constable & Robinson. She left a full-time ...reer in journalism to turn to writing, and now divides her time between the Cotswolds and Paris. For more details, visit www.agatharaisin.com, or follow M. C. Beaton on Twitter:@mc_beaton.

Regency romance series by M. C. Beaton

Regency Scandal
His Lordship's Pleasure • Her Grace's Passion • The Scandalous Lady Wright

The School for Manners
Refining Felicity • Perfecting Fiona • Enlightening Delilah
Finessing Clarissa • Animating Maria • Marrying Harriet

The Poor Relation
Lady Fortescue Steps Out • Miss Tonks Turns to Crime
Mrs Budley Falls from Grace • Sir Philip's Folly
Colonel Sandhurst to the Rescue • Back in Society

A House for the Season
The Miser of Mayfair • Plain Jane • The Wicked Godmother
Rake's Progress • The Adventuress • Rainbird's Revenge

The Six Sisters
Minerva • The Taming of Annabelle • Deirdre and Desire
Daphne • Diana the Huntress • Frederica in Fashion

The Travelling Matchmaker
Emily Goes to Exeter • Belinda Goes to Bath • Penelope Goes to Portsmouth
Beatrice Goes to Brighton • Deborah Goes to Dover • Yvonne Goes to York

Also available

Edwardian Murder Mysteries
Snobbery with Violence • Hasty Death • Sick of Shadows
Our Lady of Pain

Her Grace's Passion

M. C. Beaton

Constable • London

CONSTABLE

This paperback edition published in Great Britain in 2014

Copyright © M. C. Beaton, 1991

The moral right of the author has been asserted.

A CIP catalogue record for this book
is available from the British Library.

ISBN: 978-1-4721-1197-5 (paperback)
ISBN: 978-1-4721-0146-4 (ebook)

Typeset by TW Typesetting, Plymouth, Devon.
Printed and bound in Great Britain by
CPI Group (UK) Ltd, Croydon, CR0 4YY.

Constable
is an imprint of
Constable & Robinson Ltd
100 Victoria Embankment
London EC4Y 0DY

An Hachette UK Company
www.hachette.co.uk

www.constablerobinson.com

1 3 5 7 9 10 8 6 4 2

Contents

ONE

Matilda, duchess of Hadshire, knew she was losing her looks but did not greatly care, so deep was her misery. Her dislike of her husband had turned into hatred, a hatred that ate into her very soul.

The duke was a great collector and he had collected Matilda, much in the same way as he collected various fine and rare *objets d'art*. She had been, until lately, as pretty as a piece of Dresden, with white-fair hair and large blue eyes, a trim figure, and a faultless dress sense. For a while she had been comforted by the friendship of Annabelle and Emma, both unhappily married as well. But Emma had married the Comte Saint-Juste after the death of her husband, and Annabelle, the Earl of Darkwood, after the death of *her* husband. Both were now blissfully happy and Matilda felt cast out into a sort of outer darkness.

All the winter long she had been incarcerated in the duke's stately home in the centre of Hadshire, a small county that bordered on Gloucestershire. Ramillies Palace was a huge building, built by the third duke to celebrate his success at that famous battle against the French in 1706.

The month was May and the duchess was walking aimlessly through the formal gardens. Sunlight was glittering on flowers and trees after a recent shower, blossoms drifted around her on the lightest of winds, and on a branch high above her head, a thrush sang out an anthem to the glory of the morning.

None of this beauty penetrated the blackness of Matilda's soul. The duke had lost interest in her shortly after their marriage, having found fatal flaws in this beauty he had made his duchess. Despite her delicate and fragile appearance, Matilda had a tough, almost masculine mind, and a deep voice and forthright manner. He had never had any romantic feelings toward her, and such sexual ones as he had felt for her had quickly died. But he was, or had been, proud of her appearance. Now that misery had dimmed her beauty, he looked at her as if she offended his very soul. Objets d'art that had cracked or been found to be fakes were relegated to the attics or smashed. The duke often looked as if he would like to smash his wife. Had he ignored her very existence, then life would have been tolerable. Ramillies Palace was enormous enough for a couple not to see each other from one week's end to the next. But the duke knew his presence gave his wife pain and so he

2

kept her close. He slept late, and Matilda had come to enjoy the freedom of the mornings.

Not that she particularly needed to be out this morning, for the duke had surprised her by leaving for London and taking his brutish valet, his constant shadow, Rougemont, with him. He had now been gone for three weeks and had not written to tell her when he meant to return.

But as she approached the great house, she feared a trick and that he might be there, waiting for her.

She had no friends in the county, the duke having choked off any calls. She had learned not to become too friendly with the tenants, for the duke would find out and punish them by raising their rents. There were no servants in the huge staff who would dare to show her any warmth or interest. They had all been hand-picked by the duke, even her own lady's maid. And they watched her. They watched her constantly, for the duke encouraged them all to spy on his wife. She remembered the time on one of her walks when she had come across a small child who had fallen out of a tree. She had carried the child home and had been entertained by the grateful parents. The warmth of human company had been so wonderful, she had forgotten for the moment about her husband. She learned that the next day the family had been evicted from their cottage.

Matilda had rebelled. She had taken a small piece of jewellery that was her very own to the nearest town and sold it, tracked the family down to the workhouse, and given them a substantial sum of money. Of course the duke learned of it and she was kept locked in her room and half starved for a month. But the family had escaped, of that she was sure, for she had urged them to leave the county as soon as possible. Since then, she had not found the courage to make a stand on anything.

Although her husband had been absent for three weeks, Matilda was always conscious of the watching servants. She made her way to the breakfast room. The sideboard was groaning with dishes as usual, just as if there were an army of guests instead of one miserable and lonely duchess.

She tried to eat but the food seemed to choke her. Her gowns were beginning to hang on her now-spare figure.

After breakfast, she went up to her room and sat wearily down at the toilet table to brush her hair. But her new lady's maid, Betty, appeared and silently took the brush from her and began to brush her mistress's now-lank hair.

Then Matilda saw a small nosegay of flowers on the toilet table and reached out a wondering hand to touch them.

'How did these nasty weeds get there, Your Grace?' demanded Betty.

Matilda looked at them thoughtfully. It was an amateurish arrangement, a child's arrangement. 'Don't you like them?' she asked. 'I put them there myself this morning.'

Betty sniffed and continued to brush Matilda's hair. A little glow of warmth entered Matilda's heart as she looked at the simple bunch of wildflowers. Someone liked her enough to pay her a tribute. But the glow quickly fled. It must have been one of the servants and if that servant were discovered, then he or she would be dismissed. She stood up and submitted to having her gown removed and a fresh one put on. I wish I were Miss Bloggs of nowhere, thought Matilda. Then I could make my own meals and put on my own clothes and be as free as the air.

She half reached out a hand intending to take one of the flowers and pin it on her gown, but withdrew her hand quickly. She must show no particular interest in that little bouquet.

She passed the day reading and walking, a day that ended in a glorious sunset. Eating her solitary meal and waited on by two footmen and the butler and underbutler, all supervised by the house steward, Matilda began to feel freer than she had in a long time. She must not waste each day dreading her husband's return. On the morrow, she would sleep late and then perhaps take a drive out into the countryside. Provided she talked to no one, she could not bring harm to anyone. It was rather like having the plague or the evil eye, she thought.

After dinner, she went up to her room, looked at the toilet table, and stiffened. The flowers had gone. Betty appeared silently in the doorway.

'Where are my flowers?' asked Matilda.

'They had faded, Your Grace,' Betty said in a flat voice, 'so I threw them away.'

Betty began to prepare her for bed. Matilda hated

the touch of the maid's fingers against her skin. But she would not think of such unpleasant things. Tomorrow she would celebrate a day of freedom.

She found she awoke early as usual, despite her intention of sleeping late. Betty appeared promptly as she usually did, as if sensing her mistress would rather dress herself and being determined to thwart her.

The house steward was waiting for her in the breakfast room. 'His Grace has written to me with orders that preparations are to be made for a ball to be held here in three weeks' time, Your Grace.'

Matilda looked amazed. A ball! Normally her husband hated entertainments of any sort in his own home, although he was happy enough to attend balls and drums and ridottos at other houses. 'Does His Grace say how many are to be invited?'

'I believe he has written to his secretary, Mr Curtis, to that effect, Your Grace.'

How like him, thought Matilda, to leave all the arrangements down to the guest list in the hands of his servants. She thought of the many hostesses who would be thrown into a flutter at the idea of arranging a ball, but in her case, she knew she would not have a say in anything, not even the flower arrangements.

'Does he say when he plans to return?'

'His Grace wrote to say he will return the evening before the day of the ball.'

So she was to be free of him for at least three weeks. But what freedom had she, surrounded as she was by all his loyal servants? The prospect of a drive to the nearest town, Hadsborough, faded. She would be obliged to take Betty, outriders and footmen. It was another perfect day. Sun glinted on the silver urn, the silver teapot, the fine china, and beyond the long windows that looked out onto the terrace, dew sparkled on a lilac tree, heavy with blossom.

Her head ached and she could feel the darkness of depression settling down on her. Reading was her only solace. She would plead a headache and lock herself in her room and ask not to be disturbed. A day free of the prying eyes of the servants would be some relief.

She went back up to her room. Her eyes flew to the toilet table. There, as before, was a pretty little nosegay. She walked over and examined it and saw a spool of paper thrust into the centre of the flowers. She could hear Betty coming. Quickly she thrust the little piece of paper into the bodice of her gown and then, just as quickly, picked up the nosegay and hid it in the chamberpot under the bed. If Betty saw that nosegay, then she would become very suspicious indeed, for the maid would know her mistress had not been out walking that morning.

'I have the headache,' said Matilda, 'and do not wish to be disturbed this day. Leave me.'

'Then I shall prepare Your Grace for bed.'

'I am not going to bed. I am just going to sit here quietly. Go away, Betty.'

When the maid had reluctantly withdrawn, Matilda locked the bedroom door, then went through to her boudoir and locked that door as well and then into

7

the sitting room to close and lock the door that led out into the corridor. The house steward had spare keys to all the rooms, but she felt sure he would be too busy starting to plan arrangements for the ball to disturb her.

She unrolled the spool of paper. Written in pencil was a short message. 'Do You know ther is a Secret Passidge by the fireplace in your room? Press the rose.'

The letters were large and badly formed. Her eyes roamed around the room. The fireplace had an ugly, ornately carved overmantel, grapes and vines and, yes, roses. With a beating heart, Matilda approached it. Which rose?

She would try them all.

She pressed one after another, beginning to think it was all a hoax, when she saw a carved rose, down at the left-hand side near the fender. She pressed hard. There was a hideous grating sound and a door slid open in the wainscoting next to the fireplace.

Matilda thought quickly. If she was going to explore that secret passage then she would need to be quick. But she had better make plans before she rushed off. If that passage led out somewhere in the grounds, she could have a blessed time, walking about unobserved. She knew that normally when she went out for a walk, a footman was sent to keep a discreet eye on her.

She forced herself to be calm. She drew the bedroom curtains and then took one of her nightgowns and stuffed it with two pillows and some underwear until she felt it looked like a human form. Then she remembered she still had a wig that looked like her own hair. She had once, in the early days of her marriage, had her hair cut in a fashionable crop. The incensed duke had forced her to wear a wig until her hair grew in again. She found it in a chest at the end of the bed, lifted the top off a wig stand, which stood in a corner, placed the wig on it, tied a lacy nightcap on top, and put the 'head' on top of the dummy she had made with pillows and nightdress. She tucked the whole lot into bed. Then she wrote in large letters on a broad sheet of paper, 'I have taken laudanum and am not to be disturbed for any reason,' and pinned it on the end of the bed.

Matilda changed into riding dress, boots and hat – they being the most serviceable wear for exploring secret passages – retrieved the bouquet from the chamberpot in case it was found, and made her way to the passage, carrying a candle in her other hand.

The passage led to a narrow black staircase. She put the little bouquet down on the floor, raised the candle high, and searched for the mechanism that would close the door behind her. There was a carved stone dolphin on the inside of the secret door. She pressed and pulled at it until the door behind her grated shut.

Matilda started to make her way gingerly down the stairs. Why had the staircase been built? Had the wife of the third duke taken lovers? On and on it went, down and down, and then she found herself at the foot of the staircase with a long narrow passage stretching out in front of her. She walked and walked, wondering whether she would ever reach the end of it, glad that the place had been built in the last century and not farther back, say, in Tudor times. That might have meant danger from crumbling walls.

Just when she was beginning to wonder whether it would ever come to an end, she came up against a blank wall.

She held the candle up and stood looking at it. The wall was of smooth polished wood. Her eye caught a dark stain on the floor. She bent down and looked at it. Oil. She was sure it was oil. That might mean there was some mechanism that caused a door to open in the wall and that someone had been there recently to oil it.

Matilda began to press various parts of the wall but nothing happened. Her heart sank. The adventure was over. She raised the candle again for a last look and then nearly laughed aloud. At the top of the wall was a metal lever, jutting out. How could she have missed it? She stood on tiptoe and pulled it downward and the whole wall slid open like a door. Ahead of her lay a green tunnel of tall arched bushes and a mossy path. She turned and looked at the outside wall to find some way of shutting the door. But this time there was no carved dolphin, no rose, no lever. Determination to solve the mystery made her calmly start to probe the brickwork. But she could find nothing. Her candle wavered in the green gloom. She blew it out and put it back inside the door and continued her search. Her eye fell on a rusty foot scraper, but the rust, she noticed, lay not on the top, which was shiny and clean, but at the sides. She bent down and tugged it forward like a lever and let out a sigh of pure satisfaction when the door quietly slid closed behind her. Now to see whereabouts in the grounds she was. If she was in view of any of the outdoor servants, there would be no point in proceeding with the adventure.

The tangled path led on and on and then suddenly she found herself in a small glade carpeted with bluebells. To the west of the glade, the trees were thinner and she could see the jutting wing of the rustic, or servants' quarters. This then must be the wooded section to the far side of the house. She smiled. She was, therefore, well away from either being seen by anyone in the servants' quarters or the stables. If she continued through the wood, bearing east, she would soon reach the road that led to the town.

She set out walking briskly until she came to the wall of the estate. She nimbly climbed over it and dropped down quietly onto the road on the other side. After a mile she came to a signpost that said HADSBOROUGH, 10 MILES. Matilda groaned but continued doggedly. After about a mile she heard the rumble of wagon wheels. When the wagon came alongside her, she called to the driver, asking him whether he could take her as far as Hadsborough. He stopped and nodded and she climbed up beside him. The wagoner was a slow, incurious man, and they travelled into the market town in companionable silence. Matilda was grateful she had had the foresight to bring money with her and paid him a shilling before alighting in the market square.

She looked around eagerly at the bustling crowds and drew a breath of sheer gladness. Freedom! No one would recognize her, which was one of the advantages of having been kept mewed up at Ramillies.

Matilda wandered around stalls and in and out of shops, looking at the wares until she began to feel hungry. She went to the main posting house and was served with a light meal in the coffee room. She ate well for the first time in months, no longer caring about the long road home.

And then she became conscious of that familiar feeling of being watched. The hair began to rise at the back of her neck. At last she could bear the suspense no longer and swung about in her chair.

The coffee room was deserted save for one tall man, who was standing by the fireplace, surveying her. He was a commanding figure. His eyes were arresting, light green with a black ring around the iris and heavy lidded. He had a powerful, handsome face, lightly tanned, a clever, sensuous mouth, and glossy black hair worn rather long. His coat was exquisitely cut. He approached and made her a low bow.

'Do I have the honour of addressing the Duchess of Hadshire?' he asked. His voice was deep and husky.

'You do, sir,' said Matilda, after a momentary pause in which she had wondered whether or not to lie.

'I saw you once at Lady Bellamy's autumn ball,' he said. 'May I?' One hand indicated the chair opposite.

'Please do,' said Matilda, all the while wishing him in Jericho.

'My name is Torridon,' he said.

Matilda furrowed her brow. Then her face cleared. 'Ah, you are the Earl of Torridon,' she said. 'What brings you to Hadshire? Your estates are in the north, are they not?'

'I am staying with friends nearby, the Ansteys. I escaped by myself for the afternoon.' He gave a rueful smile. 'Country house life can become a trifle dull. And you, Your Grace? What are you doing all alone without husband or maid?'

'I escaped as well,' said Matilda. She leaned forward impulsively. 'I fear I must take you into my confidence, my lord. My husband is in Town. I am . . . well, in short, I am not allowed anywhere even in his absence. The servants watch me, you see. Please do not tell anyone you have seen me or I shall be in sore trouble.'

'My hand on my heart and my solemn promise,' he said, his eyes studying her curiously. There were shadows under her eyes and the eyes themselves held a haunted look.

'Will you not be missed?' he asked.

'I hope not,' said Matilda. 'I said I had the headache and wished to be left alone.'

'You have obviously friends among the servants.'

'I have no one loyal to me,' said Matilda quietly. 'I have found a way of coming and going unobserved. Oh, you must not speak of this!'

'Did I not give you my solemn promise?'

13

'You are very kind, sir, but you cannot know what it is to long for freedom. I do not criticize my husband,' Matilda added quickly, 'but he is, let us say, very protective.'

The Earl of Torridon's heavy eyelids drooped as he conjured up a picture of the Duke of Hadshire. A tall man, well enough looking, with large liquid black eyes, a straight nose, and a rather pretty little mouth. As cold as ice, however. It was rumoured he treated his wife shamefully. There were other rumours about him, dark rumours and whispers, hinting at cruelty. 'I do know what it is to long for freedom,' said the earl quietly. 'Did you walk all the way from Ramillies?'

'Not I,' said Matilda. 'A wagoner took me up.'

'Then with your permission, I will escort you home. Oh, no! Do not look so. I shall take you to the nearest place convenient for you.'

'Thank you,' said Matilda gratefully. She looked at him shyly. 'I am not in the way of conversing with people. I have two very good friends, the Comtesse Saint-Juste and Lady Darkwood, but the only chance I get to see them is during the Season, and . . .' She bit her lip.

'And provided your husband does not know of it,' he finished for her. Matilda remained silent. She could not criticize her husband to this stranger. Only Annabelle and Emma knew of her hatred for her husband.

'I shall be in London in a few weeks' time,' he said lightly. 'Perhaps we shall meet.'

14

'I do not know whether my husband plans to go this year or not.' Matilda sighed. 'Probably not.'

'Will you take wine with me?' he asked, looking at the jug of lemonade at Matilda's elbow.

She suddenly felt reckless. They were alone in the coffee room. From outside filtered the noise and bustle of the square. The coffee room was cool and dark, low-beamed and intimate.

'I should like that very much.'

He leaned back in his chair and shouted, 'Landlord!' and, when the landlord appeared, ordered a jug of claret.

'So what is so boring about your country house stay?' asked Matilda, sipping her wine.

'I am lost among the ladies,' he said with a rueful laugh. 'My host, old Sir James Frobisher, sleeps most of the day and so it is left to me to play the gallant. I am weary of examining watercolours, talking to pug dogs, and listening to endless recitals on the pianoforte. My wife enjoys such things, however.'

A shadow crossed Matilda's eyes. So he was married. But why not? And why should the fact he was married depress her?

'Will you not be missed by the servants?' he asked, misreading the sad expression on her face.

'No, because . . . well, because I have told you so much, I may as well tell you all.' She related her morning's adventures, ending with 'I do hope my helper is not discovered.'

'So we are both escaping for a little,' he said.

15

Something of the sadness in her face was suddenly reflected in his own.

'It is like living in a prison,' said Matilda. 'It is worse in the country. In Town, there are always parties or balls to go to, other faces to see, faces that do not watch me the whole time. And sometimes we go to the playhouse or to the Italian opera. I like that above all things. I can lose myself in a stage world for a little. I particularly like the plays with happy endings. Life appears to have so few happy endings.' She rested her chin on her hands, her eyes dreamy. 'Sometimes I imagine I am the heroine and after a few hours of adventures can live happily ever after.' She shook her head and sighed. 'But I am not normally so romantical, My Lord, and try to accept my life as it is.'

She glanced suddenly at the large clock that stood in the corner and let out a stifled exclamation. 'I had not realized how quickly the time had flown,' she said.

'Then come along,' he said, rising to his feet. 'I will soon have you back at Ramillies.'

He had a smart curricle drawn by matched bays. He dismissed his groom, saying he would pick the man up on his return journey. He made light conversation as they bowled along the deep green tunnels of the winding lanes where the tall hedges arched over the road. But Matilda only answered automatically. She was now in an agony of fear. If the servants had discovered her absence, then she would need to fret and worry for three whole weeks, wondering what the duke would do to her.

At last, she recognized the part of the wall she had climbed over and called to him to stop. He jumped lightly down and tethered the horses to a tree beside the road and held out his hand to her. She took it, feeling the strength of his hand, aware of the concern in his strange green eyes.

'Thank you,' said Matilda. 'I must go now.'

He bent and kissed her gloved hand. She curtsied and then turned and climbed over the wall, affording the Earl of Torridon a tantalizing glimpse of neat ankles.

Matilda ran through the woods so fast that by the time she reached the secret passage, she was clutching her side and gasping for breath.

Quickly she operated the mechanism to open the door. She slowed her pace and crept quietly onward and then upward. She had left her candle, but even if she had remembered it she could not have lighted it, having no tinderbox with her.

When she reached the door that led into her bedchamber, she groped around looking for the mechanism to open it – and then froze.

Voices were coming from the room. She pressed her ear to the door. 'There you are, Mr Budgens,' came Betty's voice. 'Her Grace is asleep, like I said. You'd best lock up the doors again afore she wakes.'

Budgens, the house steward, answered. 'I had to check. More than my job's worth. His Grace won't allow her no liberty and that's a fact. Strange ways. But that's the quality for you.'

Matilda, listening hard, heard their voices retreating and then the sound of the door being locked. Still, she waited, fearing some trick. Then she found the dolphin and opened the door. Her foot struck against the nosegay. She picked it up and looked at it ruefully. She could hardly tell Betty she had picked it, as she was supposed to have been in bed all day. She put the flowers in water and put the little vase with the nosegay back in the passage. Somehow, she had to find out the identity of her helper and warn him or her not to put himself or herself at risk. Then she took the dummy from the bed and dismantled it. She did not think she would find the courage to use the secret passage again.

After half an hour, she dressed for dinner and went slowly down the stairs. She ate in solitary state as usual. Her thoughts turned to the Earl of Torridon. *He* would no doubt be sitting down with his wife, their hosts and the other guests. There would be lively conversation and then, after dinner, no doubt music and cards. He was a sympathetic and charming man. His countess was indeed lucky.

'Are we going down for dinner or not?' demanded the Countess of Torridon. 'It has been an age since we heard the dressing bell and yet you are sunk there, unchanged, in a brown study.'

'I shall be with you direct,' said the earl wearily.

'I should think so, too,' said the countess, walking angrily up and down. 'You go off without a by-your-leave and refuse to tell me where you have been. I am your wife, sirrah, or had you forgot?'

'I am not likely to forget with that voice of yours dinning in my ears from morning till night,' said the earl, his eyes flashing with sudden anger. He looked at her and she stopped and swung round to face him. How beautiful he had once thought her. He had married her five years ago. She had fascinated him with her tempestuous manner, her jet-black hair and flawless skin. But what he had thought to be a passionate temperament had proved to be nothing but bad temper. Added to that, she was barren, which, he thought bitterly, would not have mattered one whit had she not seen fit to nag him to death at every opportunity. He had made his marriage vows and now he was trapped by them. This visit to the Ansteys had been an attempt by him to see if the marriage could be repaired. But she had ruined things from the start by cleverly goading him in company so that he answered her sharply and then she would look pathetically around the other members of the company as if to say, 'See how he treats me?'

'You do not care a fig for me,' railed the countess, coming to stand over him.

He looked up at her and said quietly, 'God, how you weary me.'

She spat full in his face. He jumped to his feet and slapped her, not hard for his hand stayed its force just before the impact. She sank to her knees, crying hysterically.

The earl clutched his head and then rang the bell.

He told a footman to fetch the countess's maid and then waited, numb to the weeping figure of his wife. When the maid arrived he told her to take her mistress to her own apartments.

He felt guilty. He had never struck any woman before. He sometimes thought she would drive him mad. He decided that as soon as the visit was over, he would go back to his estates in Scotland. If she wished to stay in London, then she could do so on her own. At least at home he did not see much of her, for he was able to sink himself into the agricultural work on his estates. He thought briefly of the Duchess of Hadshire. He had liked her direct and frank way of speaking. Hadshire was an odd stick, but surely no marriage was the hell that his own had become.

The earl summoned his valet, dressed quickly and went downstairs to join the Ansteys and their other guests for dinner. The ladies were clustered around the countess when he entered, and they all looked at him with horror and reproach. What appeared to be an ugly bruise marked his wife's cheek. His guilt fled and his anger rose again. He dipped a napkin in a water jug and approached his wife. Holding her firmly by one shoulder, he scrubbed at the 'bruise'. Ink came away, staining the whiteness of the napkin. He threw aside the soiled napkin and smiled down at his wife, his eyes glittering dangerously. 'Shall we go in to dinner, my dear?' said the Earl of Torridon.

TWO

Matilda was frightened to use the secret passage again. She worried and fretted that one of the servants might have seen her in Hadsborough. No more little nosegays of flowers appeared and once more she felt friendless, despised and constantly watched. She had given up looking forward to the morning post for a letter from either Annabelle or Emma. They never wrote and she could only wonder that they had forgotten her so quickly, now that both were happily married.

The servants were busy with preparations for the ball. The state apartments on the first floor were to be used, the huge Yellow Saloon for the ball itself and the adjoining rooms for supper and cards. She had no say in anything, from choosing the supper menu to the hiring of the orchestra. The efficient house steward, Budgens, saw to all that.

The duke's return approached at great speed, the days flying by. The weather had been dull and wet, and Matilda's spirits seemed to match it. Her very appearance became as dull and colourless as the weather.

On the day before the duke was due to return, she was passing the secretary's little study. The secretary, Mr Curtis, was absent. She drifted into his room and looked idly down at the desk, which was stacked high with estate account books. But there neatly in the middle of the blotter was a list of the guests invited to the ball, a neat tick against the names of those who had accepted. A number of the neighbouring county were listed. Either the duke had become less high in the instep in inviting his hitherto despised neighbours or the secretary had been at a loss as to how to make up the numbers. She glanced down the list and then her gaze stopped at the item 'Sir James and Lady Frobisher and party'. Sir James was the Earl of Torridon's host. She remembered the intelligence of the earl's green eyes and the elegance of his figure.

Matilda heard a footstep in the passage and nimbly left the room like a guilty child, although she had every right to be there. Perhaps he might come, thought Matilda. But his wife would be with him. Still, they shared a secret, and, now she came to think of it, he, too, had seemed unhappy. She went back to her bedchamber and sat down in front of the toilet table. The weather had abruptly changed and was sunny and warm. A shaft of sunlight struck across her face, showing her the greasiness of her once-beautiful hair and the greyness of her skin. She felt dirty and gritty. Then she remembered there was a pool in the woods, in that little-used part of the gardens. She looked longingly toward the fireplace. If only she could risk using that passage again. Surely the servants were too busy with all the preparations. Even Betty had not put in her usual silent appearance.

Matilda came to a decision. She locked all the doors again and once more arranged the dummy in the bed. She lighted a candle, then opened the door to the secret passage and made her way swiftly to the outside world.

The day was beautifully warm and fresh. She hastened through the trees, looking nervously over her shoulder to make sure no one was watching her.

At last she came to the pool. It was small and deep and clear. A little stream, winding through birch trees, fed the pool at one end and then rippled out at the other. Some effort had been made to landscape the surroundings at one time, but now only flat ornamental rocks on one side of it remained, and a little carefully constructed 'ruin' of a temple on the other, dating from the last century when ruins were all the rage.

The water looked cool and inviting. She had meant for decorum's sake to strip down to her shift. But the woods were so deserted and so silent and she felt so dirty and soiled that she removed every stitch of clothing and plunged in, gasping as the icy water struck her body. She swam leisurely to and fro, remembering that when she was small she had crept away from her parents' house on summer evenings to play in the river with the village girls. For the first time, she began to wonder about clothes, about what to wear for the ball. She was letting her husband ruin her appearance. It was time to fight back. She at last reluctantly left the pool, sitting as naked as a nymph in the sun on the flat rocks, letting the warmth of its rays dry her. Then she put on her clothes again and made her way reluctantly back to the house.

As she cautiously entered the bedchamber, she heard a loud knocking at the door and a footman calling, 'Your Grace, His Grace is arrived.'

She called back that she was dressing and would be downstairs presently. He had arrived a day early.

After dismantling the dummy, she changed her clothes and brushed her hair till it shone, wondering at the same time why Betty, the maid, had not put in an appearance. And then, telling herself to be courageous, she walked slowly down the main staircase.

Budgens met her at the foot. 'His Grace and company are in the drawing room,' he said.

Company? Matilda frowned and then her face cleared. Of course, he must have brought guests with him from London. Budgens signalled to a footman, who moved quickly to the double doors of the drawing room and threw them open.

The duke was standing by the fireplace, leaning one arm along the mantle and talking to a lady who was mostly shielded from Matilda by the high back of the chair. Matilda could not remember her husband's chilly face ever looking so animated before.

He raised his eyes and stared at her for a long moment and then his small mouth curved in a smile. 'Come,' he said imperiously, 'and meet our guest, Mrs Hendry.'

Matilda moved forward at the same time the lady rose from the chair and turned to face her. She was very beautiful. She was above-average height and had glossy brown hair under quite the most modish bonnet Matilda could remember seeing. Her skin was flawless and her cheeks pink. Her huge brown eyes sparkled and her mouth, as small as the duke's, was a perfect little rosebud. But it was the expression in Mrs Hendry's eyes that startled Matilda. For it was undoubtedly an expression of triumph.

Matilda curtsied to her and looked inquiringly at her husband. 'Mrs Hendry has deigned to grace our little ball,' said the duke, 'and there will be none to match her.' He raised Mrs Hendry's hand to his lips.

Mrs Hendry snatched her hand away and said with a rippling laugh, 'La! You must not. You will have Her Grace disliking me and I could not bear *that*, for we are to be bestest friends, are we not?'

She beamed at Matilda, who smiled back reluctantly. 'Have you had any refreshment?' asked Matilda. 'Are you come from London?'

'Yes, but do not worry about me. Mirabel saw to my every comfort.' Mirabel was the duke's first name, and Matilda, who never used it, looked at Mrs Hendry in dawning surprise. It was fast being borne in on her that her husband had brought his mistress home with him. Beautiful she might be, but Mrs

Hendry was not a lady. Matilda sensed that under the perfection of dress, appearance and manners lurked a very vulgar creature. Her face stiffened with distaste and she said quietly, 'You must excuse me, Hadshire, I have various things to attend to.'

'Leave us by all means,' said the duke with a malicious smile, enjoying every minute of his wife's discomfiture.

She went back up to her own little sitting room and found the duke's valet, Rougemont, waiting for her. She shrank back a little, for she was afraid of him. It was Rougemont who was commanded to lock her in her room when the duke was displeased with her, and Matilda knew the brutish valet enjoyed exercising the power the duke gave him.

'What is it, Rougemont?' demanded Matilda.

'Her,' said Rougemont. 'That Hendry female.' His harsh voice carried only the slightest trace of French accent.

'Mrs Hendry is a guest of my husband,' retorted Matilda, 'and I am sure he would not wish you to speak of her to me.'

'No, he would not,' said the valet. 'She's making a fool of him and of you, Your Grace.'

'Who is she?' asked Matilda, curiosity overcoming the repugnance she felt for this shadow of her husband's.

'Mary Hendry was married to a haberdasher who left her five shops. She sold them and taught herself the ways of the Quality. She was angling for Lord Summers when she saw His Grace and set her cap at him. Talk of London, it was. He keeps her with him constantly and they live as husband and wife, if you take my meaning.'

'Rougemont, I do not wish to threaten you, but I must tell you that if you continue in this strain, I shall be forced to report your conduct to my husband.'

His face darkened. 'You need help,' he said, moving toward her. 'What good would it do? He would dismiss me and put another such as I in my place.'

'Rougemont,' said Matilda firmly, 'leave me. Share your dislike of Mrs Hendry with the other servants if you must. I do not wish to know anything about it.'

'Then I shall deal with it myself,' he said, throwing her a contemptuous look.

After he had gone, Matilda stood for a long time, her hands clenched into fists. Her husband's behaviour was surely intolerable. Or was it? With this light o' love to keep him occupied, he would have less time to persecute his wife. She swung round and looked at herself in a long glass. Her face was still healthily pink from her morning's swim and her hair shone from the washing and brushing. She would not let him cause her to go into a decline. She would look her very best at that ball. She would wear her finest jewels and her finest gown. For a moment, she almost seemed to see the Earl of Torridon's handsome face in front of her. But she was not going to sparkle to please a man she had only met briefly and who was married, or so she told herself.

Dinner was an agony of embarrassment. The duke seemed quite besotted with his Mary and flirted with her openly. The servants' faces were stiff with disapproval. They were more snobbish than their betters. It was every nobleman's right to persecute his wife if that should be his whim. Flaunting his mistress in his own home was another matter. Matilda bore it all with as much calm as she could. She tried to escape after dinner, but the duke commanded her to entertain Mary by playing the piano. Wearily Matilda took out her music and sat down and began to play. After half an hour, she swung round to say that she had the headache and could play no more, but the words died on her lips.

Her husband was bent over Mary Hendry's chair and he was kissing the widow full on the mouth while one of his long slender white hands was thrust down the front of that lady's gown.

Her face flaming, Matilda marched from the room. As she closed the door, she could hear her husband's mocking laughter.

Later that evening, she heard carriages arriving as the guests from London who had been invited to the ball came to stay. Betty brushed her mistress's hair tenderly that evening. Matilda found she could not like this new and sympathetic maid any better than the old model. In fact all the servants, when they saw her, looked at her with sympathy in their eyes.

And then Matilda noticed a little nosegay of flowers on the toilet table. She waited until Betty had retired and then lifted the flowers out of their little vase. A screw of paper fell to the floor. She replaced the flowers and picked it up and smoothed it open.

'It be a shame' was written in clumsy letters.

Yes, it was a shame, thought Matilda, but what could she do about it?

The Earl of Torridon sat in a corner of his travelling carriage. His wife sat in the other. They were late. She had manufactured one scene after another, saying she would not go and then changing her mind. When her much-goaded husband had shown every sign of leaving without her, she had quickly changed and joined him in the carriage.

The earl turned to face her. 'You have gone too far this evening, madam,' he said quietly. 'From now on we shall live apart.'

In the bobbing light of the carriage lamp, her face turned quite white with anger. 'You cannot do this! You are my husband.'

'I am a husband who is weary of your scenes. I have had enough. I shall travel north tomorrow. You may go on to London by yourself. My lawyers will make you a generous settlement on the understanding that you do not come near me again.'

His countess was about to burst into tears but she remembered the ball just in time. She was extremely vain and had no intention of ruining her looks by appearing with red eyes.

'I know what it is!' she said. 'You have a mistress.'

'There is no woman in my life,' he retorted, 'and after my experience with you I doubt if there ever shall be.'

She gave a pettish shrug. He was out of sorts,

that was all, she thought, with one of her lightning changes of mood. Gentlemen were prone to disorders of the spleen. She could not believe he really meant to leave her.

The earl's thoughts turned to the Duchess of Hadshire. He remembered her as a small, rather dainty lady, very subdued, but with a pleasing air of honesty. He was looking forward to meeting her again.

As he mounted the staircase with his wife, he noted grimly that the duke and duchess had stopped receiving guests and were no doubt now in the ballroom. He saw his wife pout. She liked to make an entrance, to be announced, and yet was always notoriously late.

She saw some acquaintances and left his side to go and speak to them. He nodded to one or two people he knew, his eyes ranging over the ballroom, looking for the duchess. At first he thought the lady he had shared a jug of claret with had been lying, for the duke's partner was a very beautiful woman with brown hair. Surely the duke would hardly behave in such a doting manner with any female other than his wife.

And then a little knot of people broke apart at the far end of the ballroom and he saw her, the Duchess of Hadshire. He caught his breath. She was exquisitely fair. She was wearing a ballgown of silver gauze. A heavy collar of fine sapphires set in silver was around her neck, matching the intense blue of her eyes. She was as fine and dainty as a piece of

Dresden china, from the top of her shining head to her small feet. And then she saw him. For a long moment their eyes held, and then she walked across the ballroom toward him.

'How pleased I am that you are here,' said Matilda, and, indeed, she did look so very happy to see him that he smiled down into her eyes and held her hands in his. Somehow, he was aware that his wife had noticed him with the duchess and was staring at them, and yet he wanted to go on holding the duchess's little hands in his and looking deep into her blue eyes.

'Have you a dance for me?' he asked.

'N-no,' faltered Matilda, and then her face brightened. 'Perhaps I have. The next dance is the waltz. My husband is to dance it with me, but . . . but he is so attentive to his guests, he will forget as usual.' By which Matilda meant that she was sure the duke would enjoy humiliating her by leading Mary Hendry back onto the floor again.

'Then we will wait and see,' he said. Sure enough, the quadrille ended, the waltz was announced, and before all his guests, the duke led his mistress back onto the floor.

'I see what you mean,' said the earl quietly.

Plumed and jewelled heads nodded busily as the gossips got to work. Hadshire was behaving disgracefully. Who was this Mrs Hendry? 'My dear, have you not *heard* . . . ?' And so it went on as the eyes swivelled from the duke to see how his duchess was taking it, and there was his duchess floating across the floor in

31

the arms of the Earl of Torridon and looking as if she did not have a care in the world.

Matilda could feel the strength of the earl's arm at her waist and was aware of every part of his body. Despite the sanction of the waltz by the royal princes, Queen Charlotte's sons, damned as a bunch of bonhomous thugs, *The Times* had thundered against it as an 'indecent foreign dance called the waltz'. It was quite enough, raged the newspaper, to see 'the voluptuous intertwining of the limbs, and close compressure of the bodies, to see that it is far removed from the modest reserve which has hitherto been considered distinctive of English females'.

But Matilda was learning to feel like a woman. The intensity of her feelings startled her, and she was worried he might sense them. Her fingers tingled in his and her whole body swayed toward him. The faces in the ballroom were a blur. There was only the lilting music in her ears and the feel of this man's arms about her. When the music ended and he released her, she shivered, as if cold.

'Will you save the supper dance for me?' he asked.

Matilda nodded, her eyes shining. She had forgotten about his wife. She was engaged to have the supper dance with her husband, but she felt sure that the besotted duke would take Mary Hendry in to supper instead. Matilda was bewildered not only by the duke's infatuation, but by his determination to let everyone see it.

But Rougemont felt he knew the answer, his eyes sharpened with jealousy. Once, years before, when he had accompanied his master on the Grand Tour, the duke had come across a statue in the grounds of a villa where he was staying. Rougemont, standing behind a pillar, looked round it at Mary Hendry. Yes, Mary looked like that classical statue with her hair in one of the latest Roman styles and with a small curved smile on her mouth. The duke had begged his host for the statue, had offered a vast amount of money, but his host had remained adamant. He would not part with it. And so the duke had commanded Rougemont to help him steal it. The valet remembered that night, of how they had stretched and strained with six of the duke's servants to get the marble statue from its plinth and into the closed carriage, of the flight to the border, of the duke's triumph, and of how the duke had insisted on having the statue carried up to his inn bedchamber and had gloated over it, lovingly obsessed.

In vain had Rougemont tried to lure his master out for an evening of drinking and wenching; all the duke wanted to do was sit in his bedchamber and caress that statue. The next day, intelligence reached the duke that a local landowner had a fine Michelangelo and might be prepared to part with it. Rougemont, who had manufactured that intelligence, had pleaded a fever and begged to be allowed to stay in bed. The duke had commanded him to guard the statue and had taken off. Rougemont had then gone out and found a sculptor he had approached before. He paid the sculptor a great deal of money for his work.

The duke returned in the evening, furious at

having gone off on a wild goose chase, but mollified by the thought of an evening with his treasure, the statue. As usual, he commanded Rougemont to set branches of candles near it so that he could study every line.

And then the duke noticed that the mouth appeared to sneer at him. He could hardly believe his eyes. He thought it must be a trick of the light and commanded Rougemont to move the candles closer. But there it was. The corner of one side of that perfect classical mouth, or what he had hitherto considered perfect, was lifted a trifle too high, giving the mouth the appearance of a sneer rather than an enigmatic smile. Rougemont's sculptor had done his work well.

In a fury, the duke had seized the poker and smashed it full into the face of the statue and then had commanded Rougemont to get rid of it.

So, Rougemont decided, he must find a flaw in this Mary Hendry. Her beauty was perfect and her voice, unlike that of the duchess, baby soft and with a slight lisp. Nor was her manner direct or her mind intelligent, two things the duke considered most horrible in a woman. She spoke nonsense as all women were supposed to do. She was graceful, every movement studied perfection, and she danced divinely.

Rougemont thought hard. There was one little item niggling at the back of his brain . . . something at dinner. The duke, the duchess, Mary, and their London guests had taken dinner at four in the afternoon, an unfashionable hour, but reasonable enough in view of the fact they were all to have a large supper at the ball. Rougemont had been on duty, standing behind his master's chair. He frowned in concentration. He had been covertly studying Mary, hoping for some piece of vulgarity in her table manners that might disgust the duke, but she had eaten prettily and sipped at her glass of . . . water!

Now the ladies of rougedom, or the demimonde, or of cracked reputation, or of the fashionable impure did not drink water, and Rougemont was convinced, wealthy widow or not, that Mary Hendry was about one step removed from the streets. And what bound that sisterhood together? Strong drink.

He stroked his chin and moved back into the shadow of the pillar.

As Matilda had expected, her besotted husband, deaf and blind to the conventions, led the way to the supper room with Mary on his arm. She shivered as she remembered the first two days of their marriage when he had seemed obsessed by *her*. And then he had complained that her voice was too deep and her manner of speaking too direct. Still young and used to independence, Matilda had told him not to be silly. Surely honesty and openness were assets. His manner had grown gradually chilly and then crossed the line into open dislike. He had not courted her before their marriage. He had seen her at a ball and had approached her parents. She had not said a word to him until the first night of their marriage. Matilda did not care for her own looks – blondes were not fashionable – but when still doting on her, the duke had shown her one of his favourite

Dresden figurines and said she looked just like that. But china figurines were silent and did not have minds or wishes.

'You are so quiet,' said the Earl of Torridon. 'Is it because of your husband's monstrous behaviour?'

Matilda shook her head. 'I was remembering something unhappy,' she said. 'He *is* behaving very badly, is he not? I should not be discussing my husband with you, my lord, but believe me, everyone else is talking about him. He is a great collector.'

'I do not understand.'

'He collected me,' said Matilda. 'He thought I looked like a Dresden figurine. But he could not bear my fatal flaws. I am glad I am not of china, or he would have smashed me. Everything must be perfect, you see.'

'I can see no flaw in you,' he said, his matter-of-fact voice persuading the surprised Matilda that he was not flirting with her.

'It is my voice. It is a trifle deep toned for a lady, and I am apt to speak my mind.'

'Both endearing qualities.'

His voice was husky and intimate. Matilda coloured. 'But, my lord, your own wife should be here with you. I am afraid I am behaving as scandalously as my husband.'

'I must match you in frankness. This evening I have asked my wife, nay, commanded my wife to give me a separation.'

Her blue eyes flew to meet his. 'I am sorry,' she said quickly. 'But perhaps it is only a row. Married

36

couples are often rowing, I fear, and say things they do not mean.'

'I meant it. It was well considered, well thought out. Not something I would do lightly. I made my vows in church.'

'But not a divorce? You will not be free to marry,' said Matilda.

'I have no wish to marry anyone else,' he said in a low voice. 'Once is enough.'

'It is the fault of these arranged marriages,' said Matilda. 'We are expected to live out our lives in intimacy with someone we barely knew before we met them at the altar.'

'Not in my case. I had freedom of choice. I was in love.'

'Love.' Matilda sighed. 'What is love?'

'I do not know. Perhaps it has little to do with infatuation. Perhaps liking and admiration come first, a feeling of being at ease with someone, a feeling of coming home.'

She looked at him, startled, aware, her mouth opening to say, 'But that is how I feel with you.'

She blushed suddenly and looked away. And met the cold stare of her husband, a cold, calculating stare.

The duke did not love her, he hated her, but if he thought she was enjoying the company of any other man, then he would soon find some punishment to fit the crime. Matilda shuddered.

'My lord,' she said, 'I do not dislike your company, rather I enjoy it. But I am paying you too much attention and my husband has noticed the fact and will punish me.'

'But how can he?' demanded the earl wrathfully. 'Surely his own behaviour is such that he has no right to criticize you!'

'You do not know him. I have enjoyed speaking to you and wish we could meet again, but I fear after this evening, that is not possible. I should not have discussed my husband with you. I *will* keep saying that and yet when I see you, I go ahead and do it,' said Matilda ruefully. 'I keep hoping there is some way this odd marriage might work. One must try.'

'I myself have tried and tried,' he said wearily. He remembered three months before coming south, he had gone to his wife's bedchamber and given her a diamond necklace, diamonds of the finest water. She had thrown her arms about his neck and drawn him to her bed. He had made love to her, willing her to change, hoping that the scenes and tantrums would cease. But after their brief intercourse was over, she had spat at him and said he disgusted her.

Both the earl and Matilda sat silent, each wrapped in miserable thoughts until the orchestra started playing in the ballroom again, reminding both that the world went on, reality was waiting for both of them, and it was a reality in which their brief fleeting comfort in each other's company had no place.

But as the ball drew toward its close, he had a longing to see her one more time, somewhere he could speak to her freely.

He waited his opportunity. When the duke led

Mary off to the card room and his wife was busily engaged in dancing the quadrille with a young captain, he approached her and whispered, 'Meet me tomorrow.'

'Where?' demanded Matilda, half afraid, half exhilarated.

'Somewhere where we will not be seen.'

Matilda thought quickly.

'There is a pool in the grounds. If you climb over the wall where you left me that day and walk through the wood you will come to it. I shall be there at ten in the morning.' Her partner came to claim her for the next dance and she moved away.

The earl smiled to himself. He would see her again. He would look forward to that moment and forget about all his other cares.

THREE

Matilda slept uneasily. She had lain awake for a long time, dreading that her husband might send Rougemont to punish her.

She awoke at nine. She had told Betty she did not plan to rise until the afternoon and hoped the maid would not put in one of her sudden appearances.

She dressed hastily in a morning gown consisting of a silk slip under an overdress of white Brussels lace trimmed with blue ribbons. Matilda hesitated in front of the mirror. She felt she looked too, well, bridal. She had never worn the dress before, having been keeping it for some grand event. She put the dummy in the bed and quietly made her way through the secret entrance to the gardens outside. A pale-blue sky stretched overhead. Mist was winding round the boles of the trees. It promised to be a hot day.

'I should not be doing this,' said a voice over and over again in her head.

She reached the pool and sat down on a flat rock in the sun and looked at the tranquil dark water. She had a premonition of disaster, and yet what could happen to her? Her husband was no doubt sleeping in the arms of Mary and would not rise until late. He had said nothing to her after the ball. But she knew he enjoyed cat-and-mouse games and liked to punish her when she was least expecting it.

A slight breeze ruffled the delicate green leaves above her head. She grew even more nervous. Time was passing and yet there was no sign of him. What could be keeping him? Or had he realized the folly of it all and decided not to come? Why had she accepted the fact that his marriage was over so easily? And why did she automatically assume that the break-down in that marriage was his wife's fault?

The Earl of Torridon rode hard toward the duke's estate. He had been delayed, and delayed for a reason he could not have expected. Before retiring for the night, his wife had visited his room. He had eyed her narrowly, expecting a scene. But she had sat down quietly and had said, 'Before you decide to leave me forever, there is something you should know.'

'And what is that?' he had asked cynically.

Her voice, unusually low and even, answered him. 'I am with child.'

'How convenient,' he said dryly. 'And why did you not tell me of this before?'

'I wanted the right moment,' she said wearily, putting her hand to her brow. 'You must understand, my condition upsets my nerves and I become tetchy and unreasonable. I visited the physician in Hadsborough yesterday and he confirmed my suspicions.'

Still he would not believe her. Countesses did not visit physicians in small market towns. The physician called on them and attended to them in the comfort of their homes or wherever they happened to be staying. It could not be possible. And yet he had lain with her the night he had given her the diamonds.

'I know I am a wearisome burden to you, Torridon,' she said, still in that quiet tone of voice, a tone he had never heard her use before, 'but I could hardly believe the news myself. I was going to tell you when we were quiet together, sometime after the ball.'

'What is the name of this doctor?' he demanded harshly.

'Dr Ferguson.'

'You must realize, madam, in view of your scenes and tantrums of this night, I find it hard to believe you.'

'Ask the doctor if you wish,' she said sadly. 'He is a good man and will not lie to you.'

She rose to her feet, steadying herself against a chair back. 'I shall retire now, Torridon,' she said.

He instinctively moved forward to help her from the room, and she leaned against him and smiled up into his worried face. 'So we will stay together?' she asked.

'If what you say is true,' he said in a neutral voice, 'then we will stay together.'

She kissed him gently on the cheek and moved softly away into her room.

He did not sleep. He went out early, barely noticing the glory of the morning, and rode hard to Hadsborough. After finding the doctor's house, he roused the physician, apologizing for the unexpected call.

The doctor led him into a small parlour. He was an old Scotchman, a venerable-looking gentleman with a soft, lilting voice.

'I am Torridon,' said the earl. 'I believe my wife visited you yesterday.'

'I had the honour of being consulted by her ladyship, yes.'

'And is she with child?'

'I should say there is no doubt about it,' the doctor said calmly.

'But how can you tell? And for how long?'

'I would estimate about three months.'

Three months ago! That was that night, the last night he had lain with her.

Still, he persevered, unwilling to believe it. 'My good man, surely no physician can tell a woman whether she is three months pregnant or not.'

'My lady told me she had not had her monthly bleeding, if you take my meaning, my lord. Also, she has been sick in the mornings, in fact, was sick when she visited me yesterday morning. I have treated many, many ladies in my time. I should say there is no doubt.'

And so now he was riding to keep his appointment with the duchess. He had always longed for a child, and yet he felt exactly as if a trapdoor had come down on his head, locking him in a dark dungeon.

He dismounted at the estate wall where she had climbed over, tethered his horse to a tree, nimbly scaled the wall, and began to hurry through the trees.

She was sitting on a flat rock by the water, the lace of her dress spread out about her. The sunlight was shining on her silver-fair hair. She looked delicate, beautiful, ethereal – and out of reach.

He walked forward and sat down beside her and stared at the water.

'So you are come,' said Matilda, breaking the silence and looking uneasily at his tense face.

'Yes, I promised to see you. Did your husband punish you?'

'Not yet,' said Matilda. 'But he likes to wait and pounce. Why are you so unhappy, Torridon?'

She put a small hand on top of his and looked up into his face.

How blue her eyes were, he thought, and how soft her mouth. He put both hands on her shoulders and then roughly jerked her into his arms and kissed her long and deep. There was an urgency and desperation in that kiss, and Matilda answered with rising passion, feeling his lips against her own, his body against hers, the warmth of the sun on her back, feeling his passion mount to meet her own until they were clutched together like a drowning couple.

When he finally raised his head, she said with a

half sob, 'We must make plans. We must go away together. Far away. To Naples. Would you like Naples? I have never seen it. We would be together. No one would be able to come between us. No one–'

He put a hand over her lips and looked at her with a world of sadness in his green eyes.

'I cannot leave,' he said. 'My wife is with child. She told me last night and the physician confirmed it this morning.'

Matilda jerked herself out of his arms and rose to her feet. 'You – you – you,' she stammered. Then she turned and ran away from him through the trees, her small feet making no sound on the grass.

He watched her go until the last flicker of her white gown disappeared among the trees. Why had he kissed her? Because, he told himself wearily, she represented everything he had ever longed for. He had been kissing goodbye, not only to her, but to a life of love and freedom.

Matilda crept into her bedchamber, a great tiredness making her stumble. Men! They were all the same. In that one glorious moment, she had believed he loved her, but he had decided she was easy game, that was all. The day ahead had to be faced. Her husband and Mary Hendry and the guests who had stayed on had to be entertained.

She looked at the clock. Eleven in the morning and yet she felt she had spent a lifetime in the woods, a lifetime of rejection and pain.

Too depressed to think any longer, she fell asleep,

facedown on the bed, and did not wake up till Betty entered to rouse her and tell her the duke was demanding her presence. She blinked and looked at the clock. Four. He would be expecting her in the drawing room before dinner.

She stood miserably while Betty took out an evening gown and then brought forward her jewel box to select items to match the gown.

I feel like a doll, thought Matilda, being taken out of its box and put in another robe before being carried down to be shown off to the company.

She entered the drawing room half an hour later. The duke was bent over Mary, who was sitting in a chair, smiling up at him. He did not even turn his head. There were various couples standing or sitting or promenading about the long room. She stood and talked to a Mr and Mrs Kirwan. She remembered they lived locally, near Hadsborough, and had once called but had received such a chilly reception from the duke that they had not called again. They were a plain, respectable couple who talked to Matilda in hushed and sympathetic tones as if someone had died, their eyes constantly sliding to where the duke was paying court to his mistress.

Behind the couple, in a corner, stood Rougemont, ever watchful. Matilda saw the way he looked at Mary and shuddered. At least Rougemont had never hated *her* with such passion.

Dinner was announced. The air of embarrassment in the room was almost tangible. For without even looking at his wife, the duke held out his arm to Mary and led the way through to the long dining room where the table glittered with gold plate.

Matilda was seated next to Mr Kirwan with a local squire, Sir Harry Burke, on her other side. Both men vied with each other to engage her in conversation as if to keep her mind off the scandalous behaviour of her husband.

She answered each automatically, picking at her food and taking little sips of wine. Mary, Matilda noticed, was drinking lemonade. Matilda had also noticed that Rougemont had brought that jug of lemonade into the dining room and had given it to a footman to serve to Mary. So I was wrong, thought Matilda. Even Rougemont is won over.

Mary sipped at her glass of lemonade. Her eyes flirted with the duke while all the time her mind was making busy calculations. If she played her cards right, then the duke would find some way to get rid of his wife and then this could all be hers, the palace and the town house in Grosvenor Square. She looked down the long table to where Matilda sat at the other end. The duchess was wearing a pearl tiara in her fair hair and round her neck was a rope of the finest pearls. I'll make sure she takes none of that jewellery with her, thought Mary. The lemonade was very pleasant to drink and had been flavoured with liquorice. She drained her glass and signalled to the footman to refill it.

Mary began to enjoy a feeling of power. Here she was, Mary Hendry, risen from serving wench to marry a rich haberdasher, then to comfortably off widow and now on the brink of becoming a duchess. For had not the duke more or less said he would like to be free of his wife?

The more lemonade she drank, the more she wanted. She felt happy and elated. 'I cannot wait for this night,' whispered the duke in her ear.

'Oh, go on with you,' giggled Mary, and nudged him in the ribs.

A shiver of distaste crossed the duke's face, but Mary did not notice it.

She leaned and whispered to him, a very loud whisper, 'Your duchess is looking right Friday-faced and I can't say as how I blame her. Little nose proper put out of joint.'

She gave a happy laugh, which sounded in the duke's ears like the cawing of a crow. He could not think what had happened to his beloved Mary's normally dulcet tones. Her voice now held a common whine.

The covers were removed and the nuts and fruit put on the polished wood. The footmen moved deftly about with decanters of tokay, claret, port, madeira, canary and brandy.

Mary was determined to have something 'decent' to drink. She had drunk nothing but lemonade during the meal. She *deserved* a proper drink. She accepted a glass of brandy from a footman. Ah, that was better. She could feel the fiery liquid coiling about her stomach. She was invincible. She was the most beautiful woman in the land.

Matilda saw her husband was glaring down the

table at her. He gave a little jerk of his head. She promptly rose to her feet as a signal that the ladies should leave the gentlemen to their wine.

It will soon be me, thought Mary. I will soon be the one to lead the ladies from the room.

Once in the drawing room, Matilda went straight to the piano and began to play. The others talked to each other in low voices, all ignoring Mary.

Mary's elation fled. She began to become angry. She herself played the piano indifferently but prided herself on her singing. That music teacher she had hired to train her voice had begged her not to perform in public until she had more lessons, but all at once Mary was determined to startle the duke with her performance.

No sooner had the duke and the rest of the gentlemen entered the room than Mary loudly announced her intention of singing. She demanded an accompanist. Matilda, who had just risen from the piano, sat down again with a resigned air. 'What have you?' demanded Mary, leaning over her shoulder. She smelled strongly of brandy, and of the liquorice smell of arrak. Matilda wrinkled her nose. There had been no arrak served at dinner.

She spread out the sheets of music on her lap.

'That'll do,' said Mary, pointing to 'Believe Me, If All Those Endearing Young Charms.'

Matilda's fingers rippled expertly over the introductory bars. And then Mary began to sing.

Matilda's fingers faltered on the keys as she heard that voice and then she rallied.

Mary's voice cackled and shrieked, murdering the lovely ballad Thomas Moore had written for the marriage of the Duke of Wellington. What had the Duke of Wellington said when he had seen his future bride at the altar after so many years? 'By George! She has grown ugly.' Was that, wondered Matilda, what her fastidious husband was thinking?

At last Mary finished singing. There was a polite spattering of applause from all except the duke.

The Duke of Hadshire sat as if turned to stone. Only his eyes seemed alive with malignancy as he looked at Mary.

Mary met that stare and, tipsy as she was, she felt herself turning ice cold with dread. What had she done? She walked over to him and held out both hands to him. He turned away from her and said in a low voice, 'Get to your room, madam. I shall speak to you later.'

Tears started to Mary's eyes. She blundered her way out of the drawing room. Her maid, Nancy, was waiting for her in her bedchamber. 'You been at the bottle, mum?' said Nancy.

'I drank lemonade at dinner,' said Mary, 'and one brandy. Faith, one brandy, Nancy!'

'You didn't ought to have done that,' said the maid. 'You said you was going to be ever so careful.'

'Stop preaching, you bitch,' roared Mary. 'How dare he look at me so? Who does he think he is?'

There was a soft scratching at the door. Nancy opened it. Rougemont stood there with a bottle of white brandy on a tray and two glasses.

'His Grace's compliments,' said Rougemont, handing Nancy the tray, 'and he will join Mrs Hendry shortly.'

Mary's spirits soared dizzyingly. All was not lost. 'Make yourself scarce, girl,' she said to Nancy.

'Don't you go drinking any more,' warned Nancy.

'When he has sent me the best Nantes brandy? Off with you.'

Nancy bobbed a curtsy and left. Perhaps it was for the best, thought the maid. When madam was in her cups, it was easy to steal a few trinkets and take a few gowns and persuade madam the next day that she had given them away. Like many lady's maids, Nancy was very vain and coveted her mistress's clothes and jewels.

Mary drank several full glasses of brandy while she waited. He did not come. The great palace fell silent. A huge moon shone outside. She drank another glass and decided to go to his room, persuading herself that was what he had meant.

He was lying in his great bed as calm and as still as an ivory statue. Behind the great four-poster bed crouched Rougemont, waiting and listening.

Mary swayed toward the bed. 'Wake, sweeting,' she cried. 'I am come!'

The duke's eyes snapped open. Moonlight streamed into the room. He saw Mary standing there and experienced such a feeling of revulsion, he thought he was going to be sick. He struggled up against the pillows and said in an even voice, 'Get out of my room, nay, get out of my home. You *nauseate* me.'

Momentarily sobered by the venom in his voice, Mary stepped back a pace. The duke lighted the candle beside the bed. Looking more composed, he faced his mistress. 'I have no more interest in you,' he said. 'I expect you to be gone by the time I rise in the morning. You may find your way on foot. I am not going to have one of my carriages soiled by your low and common body. For you *are* low and common, are you not? Dear God, when I think of that performance in my own drawing room this evening – caterwauling and screaming like an alley cat.'

It was a wonder that the ghost of Mary's late husband did not rise from the grave to caution him, to warn him of what Mary was like in her cups. Her beautiful eyes narrowed to an angry glitter. 'Oh, no, my fine duke,' she said, 'you are not going to turn me out. We have been lovers and so I shall tell your little wife.'

'She knows,' he said. 'And now that I have endured enough of your sickening and low and vile presence, I shall ring for Rougemont to send you packing.'

He pulled himself up and reached for the bell rope.

Mary saw a thin stiletto lying on the bedside table. The duke used it as a letter opener. Quick as a flash she caught it up and held it to his throat. 'No, you don't,' she said softly.

Unaware of what was happening and maliciously enjoying her downfall, Rougemont stayed where he was. The duke did not cry out for help. He did not think for a minute she would use the knife. His eyes glinted maliciously in the candlelight. 'I ignored the gossip about your low background,' he said, 'for I could not believe it true. But you revealed yourself in your true colours this evening. You, my darling, are as common as the barber's chair.'

He smiled at her, slowly, mockingly, and reached for the bell rope.

She plunged the dagger straight into his throat.

'Take that!' hissed Mary.

Rougemont stiffened. He felt in his pocket for the pistol he kept ready primed on his master's instructions. He moved slowly round the bed. Mary was backing away, a hand across her mouth, her eyes dilated. Rougemont looked down at the bed, one quick agonized look, and then he raised the pistol and fired, hitting Mary in the heart. The shot echoed out of the room and along the corridors.

The servants came running, first one, then another, then the guests and then Matilda. All clustered around the door of the room. Rougemont was on his knees beside the bed, tears streaming down his face, holding one of his master's lifeless hands. The duke lay, a knife sticking out of his throat, his nightgown and the coverlet stained red with his blood.

For the first time in her life, Matilda, the resolute and practical Matilda, fainted dead away.

The week before the duke's funeral was like a nightmare. Matilda moved numbly through all the duties she had to do – getting rooms ready for the duke's heir, his cousin, Jeffrey Manson, and his family, interviewing the bishop about the funeral service, accepting calls from the local gentry, and beginning to answer letters of condolence that arrived by every post.

There was a letter each from Annabelle, the Countess of Darkwood, and Emma, Lady Saint-Juste. They begged Matilda to stay with one or other of them. They said they had written to her frequently but had received no reply. The duke, Matilda realized for the first time, must have collected the letters himself and destroyed them. She could not mourn her husband; in fact, the relief that he was dead made her feel acutely guilty.

And then Sir James and Lady Frobisher came to call. They asked, as so many asked, if there was anything they could do to help, and Matilda answered, as she had answered the other sympathizers, that she had all the help she needed from a large staff of servants. They stayed only fifteen minutes and when they were rising to leave, Matilda found herself asking in a strained voice, 'Are the Earl and Countess of Torridon still residing with you?'

'No,' said Sir James. 'They left yesterday afternoon, quite suddenly. Lady Torridon is with child and they are understandably in high alt. They have gone on to London.'

For the first time since her husband's death, tears stood out in Matilda's eyes. Misreading her distress, the Frobishers pressed her to come live with them once the funeral was over, but Matilda rallied with an effort and said it was her duty to see the new duke and his family settled before retiring to the dower house.

After they had left, she sat listlessly, feeling she could not go on. But the new duke arrived and she rose to welcome him. He was in sharp contrast to her late husband. He was a large, coarse, beefy man with a squat ugly wife and a noisy brood of seven children of various ages who immediately began to run through the long rooms, playing hide and seek.

'Like a mausoleum, this place is,' said the new duke. 'All those fiddly things in glass cases! I'll soon cheer it up. You are welcome to stay with us for as long as you wish, Duchess.'

A resounding crash echoed down from the Long Gallery. Matilda wondered which of her husband's prize objets d'art had been smashed by the rowdy children.

'You are very kind, Hadshire,' she said, 'but I shall be comfortably off in the dower house. It is already being aired and fired. I shall move there immediately after the funeral.'

The new duke and his wife looked relieved, particularly his wife. She longed to transform the place into something 'more cheery', as she described it to herself, without interference from another woman. Matilda pleaded the headache and went up to her bedchamber. Betty appeared as usual and stood waiting.

Matilda picked up a sealed letter from the toilet table and handed it to the maid. 'You will find, Betty,' she said, 'that I have given you an excellent reference.'

'Never say you are getting rid of me,' cried Betty.

'I am giving you your marching orders,' said

Matilda in a flat voice. 'I shall hire my own servants from now on. You may apply to the new duchess for employment if you wish. I want you to leave by the end of the week. You were my husband's creature, Betty, and you enjoyed spying on me and reporting my movements to him. From now until you leave, do not come near me again. I am well able to dress myself.'

Betty burst into noisy tears, pleading she had been loyal and devoted. Matilda remained unmoved. She rang the bell and when the butler answered its summons, she told him to take the maid away.

Then her eye fell on another little posy of flowers. There was no note this time. Matilda, despite her misery, wished she could find out the identity of this one person who cared for her welfare.

She rose early the next morning and, instead of going downstairs for breakfast, she hid in the secret passage and waited.

She was just about to give up her vigil when from the garden end of the secret way she heard the sound of the door being opened. She stood in the darkness and waited. There was a light patter of feet. She pressed herself against the wall. Then the door to her bedchamber grated open and a small figure darted in. Matilda slowly followed and stood watching.

A little boy with a mop of fair hair was bending over the toilet table with a nosegay of flowers.

'Who are you?' asked Matilda.

He swung about with a gasp of fear.

'Do not worry,' said Matilda gently. 'I will not harm you. I repeat, who are you?'

'Peter Bennet,' said the boy, standing with his head bowed. 'I am the lamp boy, Your Grace.'

Matilda remembered him. He normally wore a plain dark livery. It was his job to fill and trim all the lamps in the great house.

'Well, Peter,' said Matilda, 'I am indebted to you for the knowledge of the secret entrance to my room. But you need not creep about any longer. I am moving to the dower house after the funeral. I wish you to come with me when I leave. Would you like to be my page?'

The boy's grey eyes glowed with adoration. He bent on one knee. 'Oh, yes, Your Grace.'

'Then be off with you. Say nothing to the other servants in case they harm you. You may rise.'

'But they was talking in the servants' hall about which ones would be going with you,' said Peter.

'None except yourself,' said Matilda grimly. 'Go about your duties.'

'Yes, Your Grace.' The boy made for the door.

'Not that way,' said Matilda. 'You may use the secret way for the last time.'

She watched his slight figure disappear and smiled slightly. She would begin a new life, new servants, new home. But her spirits plunged again. All her guilt over her husband's death came flooding back. She should have tried to love him. She should not have wished for his death.

There came a scratching at the door and Rougemont

walked in. 'What do you want?' demanded Matilda harshly.

'I have come to say goodbye,' said the valet, hanging his head.

'It is of no concern,' said Matilda, turning away.

'Not to you, Your Grace,' he said in a low voice. 'I treated you cruel. But I cannot rest. I have the master's death on my conscience.'

'It had nothing to do with you!'

'Yes, it had, Your Grace. I saw that Mrs Hendry only drank water, and I knew it odd for one of her kind so I put arrak in her lemonade at dinner to make her tipsy. I knew if the duke could see her as she really was, then he would take a dislike to her. I never meant such a terrible end. I thought perhaps we could go back to our old life. We used to travel a lot and have great larks. I was devoted to His Grace.'

'Where will you go?' asked Matilda.

'Probably to sea, Your Grace. My life is ruined.'

He did indeed look a broken man but Matilda could feel no pity for him.

'Then get you hence,' she said. 'Have you been paid?'

'Yes, Your Grace.'

'By whom?'

'By the master two days before he died.'

'Then there is nothing to keep you here.'

'No, nothing,' said Rougemont sadly.

Matilda watched her former persecutor leave the room.

All at once she wanted to get out into the fresh

air. No one followed her and she knew no curious eyes were staring down from the windows. She walked through the grounds until she came to the dower house, which was a mile away. It was a square box of a place containing all the pieces of furniture, ornaments and paintings that had displeased the duke's fastidious eye. We have all failed him, thought Matilda ruefully as she looked around. He must have longed to put me here with the rest of the stuff that offended him.

The house consisted of a square hall on the left of which was a saloon and on the right, a library. On the first floor was a square light drawing room, a dining room and another saloon. On the second floor were four bedchambers and above them the attics. There was much to do, she thought. She would need to drive into Hadsborough and engage servants, buy a carriage, engage a gardener. She knew she would have a generous allowance under the duke's will, for his lawyers had already discussed it with her. One more stepping-stone and that was the funeral.

The day of the funeral was grey and a fine drizzle fell on the leaning headstones and springy turf of the churchyard. In the centre of the churchyard stood a large ugly marble vault, last resting place of the Dukes of Hadshire. Numbly Matilda stood as the coffin was placed in the vault and the marble door grated shut with a final sound. People spoke to her in murmurs, faces came and went, but what they said or what she said she could not remember.

After the funeral and the reception, she went straight to the dower house. The new duke and his wife were so delighted that she was leaving so promptly that they had ordered carriages to convey her belongings there. They also begged her to take servants from the palace until she found others, but Matilda refused, asking them only for the use of a small gig and pony, which she could drive herself.

In the evening Peter appeared, carrying a small bundle of clothes. 'You will attend me in the morning. I am going to Hadsborough to engage staff,' said Matilda. 'Supper has been sent down from the palace and there is more than enough. You will find the hamper in the kitchen. Take anything you want. I cannot, myself, eat anything.'

She was sitting in the drawing room. Peter looked about the dark room and then began to move about, lighting the candles; then he stooped and lighted the fire. He stood for a moment in the doorway, looking at her, tongue-tied. He longed to say that life went on, that that brute she had been married to was better off in the family vault, but could not bring himself to say anything for fear of being accused of impertinence. He bowed and went down to the kitchen.

FOUR

That summer was unusually hot for England. While Matilda lived the life of a semi-recluse at the dower house, the Earl of Torridon was back on his estates in Scotland, after a brief visit to Brighton in the south. He had not wanted to go to Brighton but had done so to please his wife, who craved elegant company, as she put it. She appeared to increase in size every day, and although she still threw frequent scenes and tantrums, he put it down to the troubles caused by pregnancy. To his surprise, she refused point blank to have a physician attend her. She had enjoyed Brighton as much as she could enjoy anything, and he had had difficulty in persuading her to move north. He had pointed out the climate would be cooler and less taxing on her nerves, but the unusual sultry heat followed them to Scotland.

His countess stood at the window of Torridon

Castle and watched him ride out. Then, with a sigh of relief, she rang for her French maid, Clarisse. Clarisse was often mistaken for her mistress, so grand was her dress and so haughty her air. She had a longing for pretty things, and lately a great many of the countess's finest gowns had come her way.

'Help me get rid of the child,' snapped the countess when Clarisse entered the room. 'It is too hot for such nonsense.'

'Very good, my lady,' said Clarisse in a colourless voice. She unfastened the tapes on her mistress's gown and helped her out of it and then proceeded to unfasten more tapes that held a cushion tied to the countess's stomach.

The Countess of Torridon was not pregnant. She had not bribed the doctor in Hadsborough to say so but had merely put on a convincing act. She had been obliged to take Clarisse into her confidence, and the clever and avaricious French maid had made the most of it, using the countess's masquerade to gain more pretty clothes for herself. 'What shall I do today?' asked the countess, walking up and down the small castle bedchamber in her shift. 'Why could we have not stayed in Brighton? The Scotch weary me – heathen savages.'

Clarisse picked up the gown the countess had discarded. It was of the finest India muslin, ornamented with a dainty sprig. There were four deep flounces at the hem. It had arrived only the other day from a London dressmaker.

'I told you, my lady,' said Clarisse, 'that most

women do not "show" until after six months. You could have put off wearing a cushion for some time.'

The countess ceased her pacing. 'I had to keep him happy,' she said tetchily. 'But we must be in London for the time of the supposed birth. When he is gone from the house, you will do as instructed and buy some pauper's newborn brat and bring it back and then we will say I gave birth to it. But it must be in London. Gossip travels like wildfire among these mountains, but in London it is different.'

'Do not worry, my lady,' said Clarisse, smoothing the gown she held with a covetous hand. 'All will be arranged.'

'I sometimes wonder why I bother with all this. But that Duchess of Hadshire, that little milkmaid, was free of her husband directly after the ball. It was as well Torridon was bound close to me.'

'Such a pretty gown,' murmured Clarisse, holding it up against herself and looking in the long mirror.

'Is there no end to your greed?' demanded the countess harshly. 'No, you shall not have it!'

Clarisse eyed her mistress speculatively and then reluctantly hung the gown away. In a few days she would return to the attack, and then the gown would be hers.

The Earl of Torridon rode along a hill track, glad to be away from his wife, glad to be away from southern society. He had read of the murder of the duke and had wondered how Matilda was faring. She was now free to marry again. He longed to see her just one more time. What a monster she must think him, a man who could court her and yet still share the pleasures of his wife's bed. That is how she must have seen it. The longing for her was like a sickness. Some days it dimmed to a faint regret, giving him some peace, but this day, it was as sharp and intense as it had ever been. He hoped she had survived the shock of her husband's murder, but he could not hope she was happy. He could not bear the thought of a Matilda entirely free of him. And yet what else could she be? She must look back on his behaviour with a shudder of distaste. In fact, it was more than likely that she did not think of him at all.

And Matilda tried very hard not to. The shock of her husband's murder had left her feeling tired and empty. At last she had the freedom she had craved, but she could not enjoy it. She would rather have had him still alive, to confront, to do battle with, to gain her freedom by her own efforts. She was plagued by a superstitious feeling that she had wished him to death, and although she told herself resolutely that such an idea was sheer nonsense, it lurked at the back of her mind through the hot, empty days of summer.

The servants she had hired were all local people who had to be trained to their various posts. She had the minimum number of servants: a butler, a cook-housekeeper, a footman, a scullery maid, two housemaids, a coachman and groom, and Peter, the page. They were a contented staff. They all had a great deal of leisure as the dowager duchess did not entertain at all and was content with light simple meals. Only Peter, the devoted page, fretted over his mistress's listlessness and loss of looks. Matilda was growing quite thin, and she had had her hair cropped short. She could not be bothered wearing curl papers at night, and so she wore her short, straight hair covered with a variety of caps.

She had had the dower house decorated, the walls being painted in light colours. But she could not bring herself to change the furniture, paintings or ornaments. They were the duke's rejects and so was she, and so she felt an affinity with them.

The garden was her great solace. She enjoyed working in it, planting a multitude of flowers and bushes and trees.

She had received various letters from Annabelle and Emma and had replied to them but had refused to go to either on a visit. Matilda simply wanted to stay in the country and busy herself in her garden and try to let the scars inflicted on her soul by her unhappy marriage gradually heal. She did not read the social news in the newspapers. Somewhere in a dark corner of her mind was a fear that she might see the Earl of Torridon's name. Any time any memory of that episode entered her mind, she quickly banished it.

One day, at the end of September when the days were ripe and mellow and the leaves were beginning to turn to gold, she was working in her garden, wearing an old straw hat and a plain gown, when she heard the rattle of carriage wheels and straightened up.

Visitors!

Her heart beat hard. She had no desire to see anyone. The callers that she had received in the weeks following her husband's death had only served to remind her of his murder. The servants all had instructions to tell anyone who called that she was not at home. She knelt down and continued to weed a flower bed, waiting for the sound of the carriage driving away.

Then she heard the sound of voices and approaching footsteps and got wearily to her feet, wondering why her now well-trained servants had seen fit to ignore her instructions.

She looked in amazement, for down the garden path came Emma and Annabelle. Emma was heavily pregnant.

'You cannot keep us away,' said Annabelle. 'Do not be angry with your servants. They did try. But our coachman saw you in the garden from his box and so we insisted on seeing you.'

Matilda hugged them both, her eyes filling with tears, a terrible lump in her throat. Her old friends seemed to belong to another world, a world free of dark dreams and guilt. And yet Emma's husband and Annabelle's had been murdered by French spies before both women had married again and happily.

Matilda led the way into the house, while Annabelle and Emma exchanged worried glances. Both were shocked at the change in their friend. Matilda, the exquisite and beautiful Matilda, was now thin and weary-looking and dressed worse than one of her own servants.

When they were seated in the drawing room over the tea tray, Annabelle said her husband was planning to take her to Paris on holiday and Emma said that she was bound for Brighton, the comte insisting that an unfashionable Brighton with the prince regent absent was just what she needed – sea breezes and no crowds of people to entertain. 'So why we are come,' said Annabelle at last, 'is to try to persuade you to come away with one of us. So which is it to be? Paris or Brighton?'

'Neither,' said Matilda. 'I go on very well here.'

Again the friends exchanged worried glances. 'You do not look well,' said Emma. 'You cannot still be in mourning for that dreadful husband of yours.'

'He was murdered last May,' said Matilda. 'Not so very long ago. I was not a very good wife to him.'

'My dear Matilda,' pleaded Annabelle, 'where is your usual good sense? No one could have been a good wife to that horror. When I was mourning Guy because I had wished him dead so many times, your practical approach to the matter helped me immensely. We should not speak ill of the dead, but there is no need to pretend to ourselves that our late husbands were not most difficult and dreadful men.'

Matilda turned her face away, tears beginning to run down her cheeks. Annabelle put out a hand, but Emma said, 'Let her cry. It is my belief it is the first time she has done so.'

They let her cry in peace and then Emma said, 'There is more to this than the death of your husband, is there not?'

Matilda dried her eyes and said wearily, 'Part of my guilt stems from the fact that before he died, I was contemplating running away with another man and living with him in adultery.'

'And what would have been so bad about that?' demanded Emma, who had become infected with her husband's insouciant and Gallic attitude to life. 'A lover would have done you a power of good. Who was he?'

'The Earl of Torridon.'

'Immensely handsome,' said Annabelle, 'but with an angry and bad-tempered wife. What happened?'

'We met one day in Hadsborough,' said Matilda in a low voice. 'I had managed to escape from the palace by a secret passage. Normally I could not go anywhere without being watched for, as you both know, the duke rewarded his servants for spying on me. In Hadsborough, I went to the coffee room of an inn for some refreshment and he was there and recognized me. I talked to him openly of my husband in a way I should not. But . . . but he seemed to care for me. We arranged to meet the morning after the ball. He – he kissed me and I said we should run away together, to Naples, anywhere where we might be together. He told me he could not. He told me his wife was with child.'

'And?' asked Emma.

'I was so disgusted and betrayed, I ran away from him. After that, the duke was murdered.'

'Let us look at the facts,' said Annabelle. 'This earl took advantage of the fact that your marriage was unhappy. He may even have been in love with you. It is not odd for men to sleep with wives they loathe, as we all very well know.'

'Oh, really?' said Matilda with a return to her old forthright manner. 'Are all men so? Would either of your present husbands take you to bed if they had a disgust of you?'

Emma and Annabelle looked at her sadly and shook their heads.

'So he was not the man I thought he was,' said Matilda.

Emma rallied. 'So because of one cruel husband and one philandering earl, you are burying yourself in the country, dressing like a serving wench, and half starving yourself. By your actions, dear Matilda, you are keeping the duke alive in your head and lending too much importance to the flirtation of a Scottish buck. I am now going to be very rude. Your beautiful hair, or what I can see of it under that depressing straw hat, is ruined, your figure is scrawny, and your face is become set in lines of sadness. Pooh! There is a world of handsome and kind men out there. You are comfortably off, are you not?'

Matilda nodded.

'There you are then! You can marry again and this time for love, not necessity. What of your own family? Why were they not here to support you?'

'The duke did not approve of them,' said Matilda with a sigh. 'He felt they were socially beneath him. He married me for my appearance, not my background. I have not seen them for some time. I did not wish to inflict his funeral on them. They live so very far away. They did write often, begging me to come home, but I could not. Perhaps I cannot help blaming Mama and Papa for having insisted I marry the duke, although both of them knew I did not like him very much even at that time. Dear friends, I am not recovered from the happenings of this year. Perhaps I might remove to London for the Little Season and meet you then.'

'You are merely putting us off,' said Annabelle. 'As soon as we leave, you will sink back into a torpor.'

'Do not nag me,' said Matilda. 'Talk of other things. Talk about your baby, Emma, and when it is expected.'

And so the friends talked. They stayed two days, two days in which they had the satisfaction of seeing Matilda begin to eat more and to laugh more, but neither could persuade her to leave with them.

Matilda eventually waved goodbye to both. But when they had gone, she found she had become restless and the miserable torpor into which she had been sunk since the duke's death had lifted. She went up to her bedchamber and studied her appearance in the glass. Her friends were right. Why should she ruin her looks and her life for two men who did not deserve a bit of it? Peter, the page, wept with relief when the butler informed him that the duchess was still eating well, even though her friends had left.

Matilda began to think about London. If she went there for the Little Season, she could go once more to operas and plays and call on Annabelle and Emma. She knew that the new duke would let her take up residence in the Hadshire town house in Grosvenor Square, but that would mean living with some of the old servants and a lot of unhappy memories. She wrote instead to an agent in London who hired a small house for her in Bolton Street, just off Piccadilly. Now that she had made up her mind to go, she found she was becoming excited at the prospect. She had not had a lady's maid since she had dismissed Betty. Now she elevated one of the housemaids and trained her for the post. The servants, all of them country people, were excited, as well, at the prospect of a visit to Town.

Soon she was ready to leave. The dower house was locked and shuttered and Matilda and her servants set out on the road to London.

November in London was cold and foggy that year, but against this gloomy backdrop, the Little Season glittered as cold and hard as hoar frost. Not since the last century had women worn so many jewels. The age of simplicity in dress was over and with it the vogue for simple coral necklaces and garnet ornaments. Diamonds, rubies, sapphires and emeralds sparkled and shone in the lights of thousands of candles as London society set out to banish the winter darkness.

And among the hardest and most glittering members of society was the Countess of Torridon. She had told her husband that the health of her baby would be endangered by the Scottish mists, and although he found it hard to believe that the unborn babe would fare better in the fogs and smells of London, he fell in with her wishes. But although she pleaded nervousness and fatigue to win every argument, she seemed to have endless stamina when it came to balls and parties. As the birth of her child was supposed to be imminent, she had a large enough cushion strapped under her gowns to maintain the fiction. She was content to sit with the dowagers at balls and parties, watching the dancers, and so it might have gone on until she finally gave birth to her cushion or, rather, cast it off and presented her husband with some pauper baby bought for the purpose by Clarisse. But then the Dowager Duchess of Hadshire appeared back in London society.

Matilda had been persuaded to attend a ball at Courtney House in Piccadilly, home of the Earl and Countess of Courtney, by Annabelle. Emma had given birth to a pretty baby girl, and she and her comte were content to remain at home. It was left to Annabelle to bring the reluctant duchess 'out'.

More for the sake of peace and quiet and a desire to please her friend than from any real desire to go to a ball, Matilda was persuaded to accept the Courtneys' invitation.

She had learned the Earl of Torridon was in London and that his wife was big with child, but the news had caused no distress in her heart. Her mind, as usual, flinched away from any thought of the earl. But she did not expect him to be at the ball, for a gossip had told her, mistakenly, that the Torridons had left town.

Matilda had been used to dressing with meticulous care when her husband had been alive, for he used to walk round her, scrutinizing her closely with his quizzing glass, to make sure she was perfect in every detail. Since the summer, her appearance had improved. Her light-golden hair was longer and she had put on some much-needed weight. New gowns had been made for her, all of the most fashionable design. The only thing that worried Annabelle and Emma was her lack of animation. There was something *frozen* about her, as if some of the November fogs had crept into her very soul.

The dress that was laid out ready for her to put on was correct half-mourning, pale-grey lace edged with purple velvet. Matilda sat down at the toilet table in her petticoat, as she preferred to arrange her hair herself. She removed her curl papers and brushed out her hair and then pinned it up on top of her head. Her maid, Esther, handed her a diamond tiara, which Matilda carefully placed on top of her head. Esther then held out a diamond necklace of five strands of gems of the finest water. Matilda nodded and Esther clasped the gems around her neck. And then Matilda heard the sound of a tambour and flute drifting up from the street below. She rose and went to the window and looked down. A shabby pair of dancers was performing below. There, leaping about was a thin, gaunt young man in a bashed tall hat, a long tail coat and black tights. His partner was a plump little girl with blonde curls, wearing spangled tights and a black velvet laced bodice. But they were in love, that unlikely pair, and their love lent them grace and beauty as they circulated to the jaunty music of the flute and tambour played by two urchins.

'Fetch my reticule, Esther,' said Matilda, without taking her eyes off the dancers. When her reticule was handed to her, Matilda fumbled in it until her groping fingers found a sovereign. She opened the window and tossed it down. It lay glittering for a moment on the frosty pavement. Then the girl stooped and picked it up and bit it in her strong teeth. She said something to the man. Then both looked up to where Matilda stood at the window, wearing only the diamonds and her petticoat. The girl curtsied and the man bowed. They nodded to the two urchins who began to play again, and then they began to perform a minuet, their oddly clothed figures moving with stateliness and grace. The fog was thickening and the two dancers moved across the frosty pavement like figures in a dream. When they had finished, they saluted Matilda again, the man put an arm about the girl's waist, and she leaned her head on his shoulder as they walked off followed by their miniature 'band'.

Matilda gave a little sigh and closed the window. Esther was standing by the bed, holding up the grey lace dress.

'I do not want that,' said Matilda with a shiver. 'It would be like wearing fog. I want something gay. Fetch me the rainbow gauze.'

The maid tried to protest. 'Folks will be shocked, Your Grace.'

'Society is never shocked. It only pretends to be. I want to wear that gown, Esther.'

Matilda had fallen in love with that rainbow gauze material and had chosen it and had it made into a ball gown with a view to wearing it in some happier and future time. After it had arrived, she had told the maid to hide it in the back of the wardrobe, wondering what could have possessed her to order such a frivolous gown when she had no intention of ever wearing it. But now, she thought of the love and happiness and, yes, brave gallantry of the dancers. She would put on an appearance of being merry and then perhaps some of it might permeate to the cold inside her that never seemed to go away.

The rainbow gauze had been fashioned into a simple gown with wide sleeves, a deep neckline, and pretty flounces at the hem. 'The diamonds are too cold,' murmured Matilda after the gown had been put on. 'Rubies, I think. Something to warm me.'

The maid brought out a small tiara of blood-red rubies set in gold filigree, gold so fine that once it was on Matilda's golden hair, only the rubies shone like drops of blood, as if without support of any kind. There was a necklace to go with it, small sparkling rubies set in the same filigree but ending in one large ruby drop that burned like fire against the whiteness of Matilda's bosom. Gold kid slippers and gold kid gloves completed the ensemble. 'What do you think, Esther?' asked Matilda at last.

'Beautiful, Your Grace,' said Esther reverently. 'But there is just one thing, if I might be so bold?'

'That being?'

'Your eyebrows, Your Grace.'

Matilda's blue eyes flashed with sudden anger and the maid drew back a pace. 'No, no, Esther,' said Matilda wearily, her anger going as quickly as it had come. 'I was thinking of something else.'

The duke had made her paint her eyebrows black, Matilda remembered. When he had briefly been besotted with her, he had said her eyebrows were like little gold and silver wings. But when disgust of her had settled in, he had expected her to be fashionable, and being fashionable meant having black eyebrows – and hairy ones, at that. Matilda shuddered, remembering the day he had bought her a pair of false black eyebrows and insisted she wear them. Fortunately false eyebrows, as every society woman knew, had a tendency to slip, and so the duke had gone back to commanding her to paint them.

When Matilda was ready to climb into her carriage, only the admiration of Peter, the page, handsome in black-and-gold livery, gave her courage. She suddenly dreaded to think what people would say when they saw her arriving at the ball without a shred of mourning on her. But the duchess who dressed impeccably for all occasions had been the late duke's creation. He would never have approved of the rainbow gauze gown. I am determined to be myself, thought Matilda, and then gloomily reflected that after having been under the duke's domination for so long, she really did not know who she was.

The fog was very thick, turning London into a black and mysterious place where carriages loomed up out of the gloom like primeval monsters, their lights like glaring eyes. Lights blazed out from the Courtneys' mansion, turning the arriving guests still out in the fog and set against its glare into two-dimensional black cut-out figures that quickly became three-dimensional as they stepped forward onto the red carpet and entered the house.

Matilda went into the dressing room set aside for the ladies and let Esther take her cloak. She nodded to various people she knew. There was no sign of Annabelle. She sat down and fiddled with her hair, hoping that if she waited long enough, her friend would arrive. The Countess of Torridon walked in. Her eyes met those of Matilda in the glass. The countess's eyes were full of venom. Matilda rose and left the room.

She mounted the staircase, wishing she had a companion with her, wishing her clothes were not quite so gaudy.

The Courtneys greeted her with such affection that Matilda was surprised. She still did not realize in all her misery that her husband had been generally detested and she herself an object of pity. No one, least of all the Courtneys, found it odd that she was not wearing any mourning.

She saw a Mrs Rochester, a lady who had been kind to her in the past, sitting with the chaperones, and was making her way around the floor to join her when she suddenly found herself surrounded by gentlemen, begging for a dance.

She accepted the invitation of a handsome colonel and joined a set for the cotillion.

Matilda was beginning to enjoy herself. The colonel was paying her lavish compliments and she was attempting to flirt with him, but feeling very gauche, for she had never dared flirt with anyone at all when her husband was alive.

And then she became aware that someone was watching her intently. She half turned her head to meet the green gaze of the Earl of Torridon. Her steps faltered. He was still handsome, but in a more satanic way than she remembered, tall, broad shouldered, his black hair gleaming in the candlelight, his tanned face hard and set. She trembled but comforted herself with the thought that he would surely not dare approach her.

But he tried. He came up to her as soon as the dance was over and bowed low. He begged the favour of a dance. Matilda was relieved to show him that her card was full. When her husband was alive, few of the young men dared ask her to dance, for all knew the duke could be spiteful, but now she was popular.

'I must speak to you,' he said urgently.

'There is your wife,' said Matilda. 'She has just entered the ballroom.' Then she turned away gratefully to her next partner.

But Matilda's earlier feeling of enjoyment had fled.

She wanted to run away and return to her former isolation. There was no sign of Annabelle.

'How vastly fetching our dowager duchess looks,' said Lady Courtney to the Countess of Torridon. 'So sensible of her not to go around dressed like a crow, for we all knew her husband to be a veritable ogre. And how beautifully she dances! Old Colonel Rogers was just saying she is a pocket Venus. She will be married again before this Season is over.'

The countess bristled. She prided herself on her own dancing. What a curse this masquerade of a pregnancy was!

She contented herself by taking a seat with the dowagers and remarking to one and all that the Dowager Duchess of Hadshire was looking very *French*. To London society French meant over-painted and bold. But she found no one prepared to lend a sympathetic ear. All had hated the duke and pitied his little wife, and all were happy to see her back in circulation.

Matilda put a brave face on it, aware always of the Earl of Torridon. She finished one dance and turned to look for her next partner, a Mr Judd, but there was no sign of him. Just before the music struck up for the waltz, she found the earl next to her. He silently took her card and then smiled. 'You should not offer precious dances to hardened gamblers,' he said. 'Young Judd is in the card room and playing deep. So my dance, I think.'

She wanted to protest, wanted to run away, but he had taken her hand in his and put his other hand firmly at her waist. Her distress fled and, along with it, her embarrassment and her disgust of him. She had a feeling of coming home, of being safe, of a lightening of her spirits, of the ice inside her melting away.

'I did not know I was already trapped when I made love to you,' he said harshly, and she looked up into his sad eyes, frightened and lost again.

'Do not look so,' he said urgently. 'I had been trying for so long to save my marriage and before we journeyed south to stay with the Frobishers, I made an effort, a last effort if you take my meaning. But it did not work, nothing seemed to work. I told her I wanted a separation and I would have told her that even had I not met you. She told me she was with child. I quizzed the doctor in Hadsborough, for it all seemed amazingly convenient, but she was telling the truth for the first time in her life. So that is how matters stood. I should never have touched you, but when I saw you beside the pool, I lost my head, thinking of what life could have been like. I am very, very sorry. Pray, accept my apologies. Surely you, above all others, know what it is to be trapped. I am breaking with convention in discussing my wife with you, but I must break the convention, do you not see, to assure you I did not, do not, regard you lightly.'

'I forgive you,' said Matilda slowly. 'And, yes, I can understand. Please do not speak of it again. I am so weary of being miserable.'

He smiled at her in such a way that her heart ached, and then he said, 'Then we shall both try to be happy.'

The Countess of Torridon watched her husband and saw the way he smiled at Matilda. She felt her heart would burst with rage and jealousy. She did not love him, but he was her property. She felt herself to be far more beautiful than the little duchess. If only she could dance!

Then she thought, Why not? The cushion was strapped on tightly. The next dance was the quadrille, and the countess had learned some new steps. She could not summon her husband and ask him to dance with her for she knew he would refuse. She saw Sir Charles Follett, a well-known fop, and signalled to him to join her.

'I have a mind to dance the quadrille,' said the countess.

Sir Charles raised his little hands, the palms of which were stained with cochineal, in horror. 'But, dear lady, your delicate condition.'

'I am very well,' said the countess. 'It is so wearisome to sit and watch the dancing and not to join in. Do say you will grant me this favour.'

Sir Charles longed to refuse; he felt that to lead a lady so far gone in pregnancy as the countess to the floor would mean he was making a cake of himself. But there was something steely in the countess's eye that reminded Sir Charles of his mother, and any woman who reminded Sir Charles of his mother could do what she liked with him.

The Earl of Torridon noticed his wife had taken the floor only after the quadrille had begun. He wanted to stop her, but knew she would make a noisy scene.

The quadrille had always been a difficult dance, or, rather, the leaders of society made it difficult. For rich women often spent a great deal of time in perfecting their dancing and music. There were delicate little misses who could play the pianoforte as well as any concert pianist. There were society women who could dance like Madame Vestris because they spent long hours under the tuition of ballet masters. Being rich meant taking one's pleasures very seriously indeed. And so the quadrille was often graced with men and women leaping about with all the finesse and elegance of the corps de ballet. The countess had been trained to perform entrechats with style, but it was her pride in this achievement that was to be her undoing.

The entrechat, that ballet leap with many crossings of legs in the air, proved too much for the tapes that held the cushion. They snapped and the cushion fell down and rolled into the middle of the set.

Sir Charles, seeing a suddenly slim countess in front of him, looked from her and then to the cushion and then back again, and began to laugh hysterically. 'I' Faith,' he cried, his voice shrill above the music. 'My lady has given birth to a *cushion*. My dear Torridon, your wife has been playing you false with a *sofa*!'

The dancers stood frozen as if some evil fairy had turned them to stone. Matilda's partner, a Mr Despard, stood with one leg raised and his mouth open. Lady Courtney was standing, her arm raised above her head. All eyes looked from the stricken countess to the furious earl.

Then the countess turned and ran from the room. The band stopped playing.

'Oh, do go on with your dance,' said the Earl of Torridon harshly. 'I have not been so greatly amused this age!'

The band struck up again and the earl walked into the supper room and called for wine. He felt he should be outraged, furious, but all he felt was the lightness of relief. She had tricked him but he was now free of her, and she had supplied him with excellent grounds for divorce. He eventually returned to the ballroom in time to see Matilda taking leave of her hosts. He followed her down the stairs and caught up with her in the hall.

'I shall escort you home,' he said.

Matilda looked at him in amazement. 'Do not add scandal to more scandal, my lord.'

'There is no one to see us,' he said, ignoring the presence of curious footmen and Matilda's maid, Esther.

'You must go home,' said Matilda. She went into the anteroom and waited while Esther put her cloak about her shoulders. Then Esther left to order the duchess's carriage to be brought round. Matilda stayed where she was, waiting. She could not be seen leaving with him. His wife had played a terrible trick on him. Society would talk of nothing else for days. The earl would be made to look like a fool.

When Esther returned to say the carriage was ready and waiting, Matilda asked anxiously, 'Is my lord still there?'

'No, Your Grace,' said Esther. 'My lord walked off into the night.'

Sighing, half with relief, half with disappointment, Matilda walked out to the carriage with Esther.

FIVE

Matilda journeyed homeward inch by inch as the carriage crawled through the suffocating fog.

'This filthy weather,' moaned Esther. 'That gown of yours will be ruined, Your Grace.'

'Perhaps it will wash. I think my cloak will protect it from the worst the fog can do,' said Matilda in a distracted way. What would he do now? she was thinking. If he leaves her, people will say it is because he prefers me. Perhaps no one noticed him following me out. And where was Annabelle?

How quiet and still London was in the fog. All sounds were muffled. All was blackness except for an occasional fire-fly flicker where some link boy led the way through the Stygian gloom.

Despite the blackness, Matilda was able to make out, when the carriage stopped in Bolton Street, that all the candles and lamps in the drawing room were still lighted.

Her butler, Smith, opened the door to her and said, 'Your Grace, the Earl of Torridon awaits you in the drawing room. My lord says you left something of value at the ball and he is returning it to you.'

'Very well. I will see his lordship,' said Matilda in a tired voice.

She climbed the stairs to the first floor and entered the drawing room. He rose to meet her. 'You may leave us,' said Matilda to Esther. 'I shall not be long.'

When the maid had retired, Matilda said crossly, 'I left nothing of value at the ball.'

'I had to see you,' he said.

Matilda faced him resolutely. 'My lord, your wife played a shabby trick on you. But have you considered the reason? You had asked her for a separation. The poor lady must have been prepared to do anything, to lie and cheat, to keep you. She must love you very much.'

'You are mistaken. She wishes to *own* me. She has no desire to be a cast-off wife, that is all. I am weary of her scenes and tantrums. At times, I think she is not quite sane.'

'I married the duke straight from the country,' said Matilda. 'I am not used to the loose morals of society. You first met me at a time when I was deeply unhappy. Please leave me alone. What your wife is or is not is not my concern.'

'If I succeed in gaining a divorce,' he said quietly, 'will you marry me?'

Matilda closed her eyes. She could think of no greater happiness than being his wife, but yet it could not be happiness if it caused another woman misery.

'While she lives, I will always think of her as your wife,' replied Matilda. 'I cannot wait for you.'

He sat down suddenly and passed a hand over his forehead. 'Then let me stay and talk to you for a little before we part. Is that too much to ask?'

'No, my lord,' said Matilda. 'We will have a short time together and then we must part forever.'

The Countess of Torridon had drunk quite a quantity of brandy and was feeling better. She was confident she could lure her husband to her bed and so save her marriage. She had never tried to seduce him before. She had fascinated him once and could do so again.

Her maid, Clarisse, came quickly into the room and began to lay out the countess's nightdress and nightcap. The countess's eyes lit with malice. Clarisse did not know yet what had happened, did not know yet that her hold over her mistress had gone.

'Ah, Clarisse,' said the countess. 'Do you recall all those gowns and scarves and trinkets I have given you?'

'Of course, my lady.'

'Then bring them all here. I want them back.'

Clarisse looked at the nearly empty brandy decanter and smiled. 'You have had too much to drink, my lady. You forget, it is in your interest to keep me happy.'

The countess, who had been seated when the maid

entered the room, rose to her feet. The maid looked in surprise at her slim figure. 'The cushion, my lady!'

'Yes, that cushion fell off at the ball, right at everyone's feet. So your power has gone. You had better bring back all I have given you. I will tell my husband how you connived to make him believe in the pregnancy and you will be out in the street by tomorrow. I will tell him it was all your idea. Now fetch those things!'

Clarisse had a small room off the countess's apartments. Too shocked to do other than obey, she went along to it and began to take all the glorious gowns and mantles from the wardrobe and the jewels from the box. Tears started to her eyes. She loved fine things with a passion. She could not give them back! And what of the morrow? The earl did not like his wife, but he would know that she, Clarisse, was party to the deception and that would be enough. No job. No reference. Nothing left to do but sink to the streets. Clarisse shuddered. Never!

She dropped the garments and quietly opened the door to the corridor and crept down to the kitchens. She searched diligently until she found what she was looking for: arsenic. As in most households, arsenic was used for keeping down rats, for making cosmetics, for making wallpaper paste to keep the bugs at bay. She spooned a quantity onto a small piece of newspaper and then rolled it into a twist. Then she darted up the stairs again and into her room in time to hear the countess shout, 'Where are you? What is keeping you?'

'Coming, my lady,' called Clarisse.

She scooped up armfuls of clothes and ran into the countess's bedchamber. 'Very good, my precious one,' sneered the countess. 'And now fetch the jewels.'

Clarisse meekly went back and collected the jewels, small brooches, single-strand necklaces, and pins, but all worth a small fortune.

'Now,' said the countess, 'you may undress me.'

With trembling fingers, Clarisse undid the tapes and pins that held her mistress's dress. There was a glass of brandy on the toilet table. Would the countess drink it before she went to bed?

Once in her nightgown, the countess sat down at the toilet table and applied white cream to her face, cleansing off the colour from her eyebrows, which she had dyed with elderberry juice, the rouge from her cheeks, which Clarisse had made by boiling Brazilwood shavings, rock alum, and red wine, and the carmine made from cochineal from her lips. She did not see Clarisse move quietly beside her and tip the white powder into the brandy glass.

'My lady should not drink so much,' said Clarisse. This, as she hoped, had the desired effect.

'Damn your impertinence,' said the countess. She reached blindly out for the glass of brandy, picked it up, and tossed off the contents. Clarisse stood back and watched.

Nothing happened.

Clarisse began to tremble. Surely she had put enough powder in that brandy to kill a cellarful of rats, let alone one unwanted countess.

'I am ready for bed,' said the countess, standing up. Clarisse turned down the bedcovers. The countess was just climbing into bed when she gave a startled gargling sound and clutched her throat. Then terrible retching noises seemed torn from her. Impassively Clarisse watched the death throes of her mistress. When it was all over she smoothed down her apron with a careful hand, picked up all her clothes and carried them back to her room, and with loving hands, hung them away again. She returned, but only to fetch her jewels. She opened the countess's jewel box and took out several of the smallest but choicest items. These she carried through to her room and hid in a trunk under her bed. She returned and stood for a few moments, looking impassively at the now-dead countess, and then Clarisse ran to the door and began to scream loudly, 'The mistress has been poisoned. Come quick!'

An uneasy silence fell between the Earl of Torridon and Matilda. She had talked of her childhood in the country and laughed over all the economies her family had undergone to keep up appearances. He had told her of going to the wars straight from school and of the campaigns and long marches, of how he had sold out when he had inherited the earldom, and of the struggle to put his estates in order. They sat in opposite chairs, not touching, but each painfully aware of the other. Bands of fog lay across the room, adding an air of unreality to the scene. The clocks chimed five in the morning and at last he reluctantly got to his feet. She rose as well.

He took her hands in his and looked down into her eyes. 'If only she would die,' he said.

'You must not say that,' exclaimed Matilda. 'Oh, I wished the same so many times, but about my husband. And then when he was murdered, I felt such shame and guilt, almost as if I had murdered him myself.'

'We will see each other again, no doubt, at one of the social functions,' said the earl.

Matilda shook her head sadly. 'I could not bear it. I shall stay as a recluse until you have left London.'

'Oh, my *darling*.' He pulled her into his arms and kissed her deeply and longingly. She wound her arms about his neck, still and motionless in his embrace, lost in it. They stood like that for a long time and then the little rubies of Matilda's tiara began to shake as she pushed him away.

'No, you must go now,' she pleaded.

'If she were dead, would you marry me?' he asked.

'Yes, with all my heart,' said Matilda. 'But she will not die and we must not wish it.'

He kissed her hand then turned and walked from the room. She crossed to the window and looked down. Although she heard the street door open and close, she could see nothing of him for the fog blotted out the street below.

The earl walked home slowly through the fog. He dreaded the scenes and tantrums that lay ahead. But he could not live with his wife any longer. He would get a divorce and then perhaps Matilda might change her mind. As he entered St James's Square, he sensed there was something up. He could not see anything but there seemed to be a great deal of turmoil from the corner of the square in which his house stood. He quickened his pace.

The door to his home stood open and, as he walked up to the steps, he saw two parish constables standing in the hall. His servants were milling about, chattering and exclaiming. They fell silent at the sight of him.

'What are you doing here?' he cried. 'What's amiss?'

The door to his library opened and the magistrate from Bow Street, Sir Henry Baxter, stepped out. 'There is sad news, my lord,' he said. 'I must tell you that your wife is dead.'

He stood there, shock, bewilderment and relief flooding his body. 'Dead. But how?'

'My lady died of arsenical poisoning. There were traces of arsenic powder in a glass in her room,' said Sir Henry.

'But she would never take her own life. Never!' said the earl.

'That is what we thought, my lord. We have already interviewed the servants. We understand you were not on good terms with your lady, in fact, had been overheard several times wishing her death. Where were you this night, my lord?'

'I was visiting a lady.'

'And the name of that lady?'

'That, I am afraid, I cannot tell you.'

'My lord,' said the magistrate severely, 'I must warn you that no one else but yourself held any ill will toward her.'

'Are you accusing me of *murdering* her? You must be mad.'

Sir Henry thought quickly. Had he been dealing with, say, Mr Bloggs of Clapham, he would have taken him into custody on the spot. But the earl had powerful friends.

'As far as you are concerned, my lord,' said the magistrate with careful deference, 'the matter can be quickly cleared up. As you had asked the servants not to wait up for you, none can tell whether you returned earlier in the evening or not. The lady's maid, Clarisse, said her mistress told her that she had been deceiving you over the matter of her pregnancy and that you had threatened to kill her. Clarisse said her ladyship retired immediately after coming home. There is no reason to suspect the lady's maid or any of the other servants. They had nothing to gain and no reason to wish the countess dead. If you have, as you say, been with a lady this night, then I must ask you again for the name and address of that lady so that we may look elsewhere in our investigations. Come, my lord, you have had a dreadful shock and you must see that, were you in my position, you would ask the same thing.'

'Do what you will,' said the earl wearily. 'But I cannot give you the name of the lady. The call was all that is respectable, but I have no wish to damage her name.'

'Then you disappoint me, my lord. I will call on you later today.'

'May I see my wife?' demanded the earl harshly.

'Of course, my lord.'

The earl strode upstairs. He opened the door of his wife's bedchamber. She was lying on the bed. Her hands had been crossed on her breast and her eyes closed. But her face was distorted and covered with blue marks like bruises. He shuddered and turned away, saying to his butler who had followed him, 'Send Clarisse to me. I shall be in the study.'

Ten minutes later Clarisse entered the study and stood with her eyes lowered.

'Now, Clarisse,' said the earl, 'tell me exactly what the countess said and did before her death.'

'My lady came back from the ball and I went to attend her,' said Clarisse, not raising her eyes. 'My lady was in a great taking, saying you had discovered her deception. She said I was as much to blame. But, my lord, she made me do it. I had no other alternative. She would have cast me off without a reference.'

'I understand. But what was her state of mind?'

Clarisse thought quickly. She had assumed the earl would be arrested for the murder, for had not she and the other servants often been witness to the couple's stormy scenes? But the earl had not been arrested, and unless she thought quickly, the authorities would begin to look elsewhere for the murderer.

'My lady cried a great deal,' said Clarisse. 'She said her life was ruined. She demanded brandy and drank a great deal. Then she dismissed me, saying she would attend to herself.'

'And did you tell all this to the authorities?'

'No, my lord.'

'Why, in God's name?'

'Suicide is a crime, my lord, before God. I am sure my lady took her own life. I did not say so at the time and I am sorry. I felt I had to protect her name even in death. I will tell them the truth.'

'You had better,' said the earl grimly. 'What possessed you to tell Sir Henry that fiction about me threatening to kill her?'

'I was distraught. I meant that in Scotland, for example, you did say, and in front of me, that you wished she were dead.'

'Hardly the same thing. You have given Sir Henry the impression that I threatened to kill her after the ball. You must tell the truth this time.'

He rang the bell. 'Is that magistrate still in the house?' he demanded.

'Sir Henry is just taking his leave,' replied the butler.

'Then catch him and fetch him here.' The earl looked curiously at Clarisse. 'You say you are French?'

'Yes, my lord.'

'And yet you have no accent.'

'My parents are French, my lord. I was schooled in England.'

She raised her eyes briefly, found he was studying her intently, and dropped them again.

'I have noticed my wife gave you many of her best clothes and some jewellery. That was no doubt to keep your mouth shut.'

'Oh, no, my lord. My lady was most fond of me.'

'You amaze me. My wife was fond of no one but herself.'

Clarisse began to cry, or to pretend to cry, but once started, she found the tears were genuine, for she was beginning to feel very afraid.

'Dry your eyes,' said the earl abruptly. 'Here comes Sir Henry. Tell your story honestly and properly so that he may not think I have bullied you into implying suicide.

Sir Henry listened carefully to the maid. Clarisse was impressive in her distress.

'Then it seems it must be as I first feared,' said Sir Henry. 'Tell me how and when you discovered your wife was not pregnant, Lord Torridon.'

The earl put his hand to his brow. 'It was at the Courtneys' ball this night. She insisted on dancing. It was during the quadrille that a cushion rolled from under her gown onto the floor, revealing not only to me but to society, the sham and deception.'

'Did you want a child very much, my lord?'

'It was not that. Not like that. My wife was much given to scenes and tantrums and excesses of rage. I did not think I could tolerate her any longer and so I demanded a separation. That was the night she told me she was with child. I am not usually so easily gulled, but she was very convincing and said she had been to a doctor in Hadsborough, a Dr Ferguson. I called on the doctor and he told me that she was indeed with child. I should have known that he could not possibly tell at such an early stage. But she was so convincing.'

'And because of the episode at the ball, would you again have demanded that separation?'

'My dear man, after what you so politely call that episode, I would have divorced her and had excellent grounds for doing so.'

'Then we must conclude that your wife committed suicide, my lord.'

'I cannot believe it,' said the earl. 'No matter what happened to her, she would never, ever contemplate suicide.'

'Of course you find it hard to believe,' said the magistrate. 'I have seen a case like this before. The husband naturally does not want to think, faced with the shock of such a death, that he may have done anything to cause his wife to take her life, but you must admit, there does not seem to be any other explanation.'

The earl looked at him wearily. Had he really caused her to take her own life? He would never know. Now he was free, but in such a manner that he could not possibly expect Matilda to marry him, ever.

Matilda received a call from Annabelle late the following afternoon, an Annabelle who made profuse apologies for her absence from the ball. 'For I had been to the physician and there is no doubt in my mind, dear Matilda, that I am to have a child.'

Matilda hugged her and congratulated her warmly. 'But,' said Annabelle at last when she had exhausted the subject of the possible sex and name for the baby, 'what of you? The drama of last night! It is all over London.'

'Ah, yes,' said Matilda. 'The countess gave birth to a cushion right in the middle of the quadrille.'

'Not only that, but found dead of arsenical poisoning!'

Matilda went quite white. 'How? Who did it?'

''Tis said she committed suicide, but gossip will have it that the sinister earl poisoned her himself.' Annabelle bit her lip and coloured. The gossips had also said that the earl was obviously enamoured of the pretty dowager duchess.

'And when did she die?' asked Matilda faintly.

'Evidently shortly after she arrived home. The earl himself did not arrive until before dawn, but he had told the servants not to wait up, so they cannot say whether he had returned home earlier and then left. The earl says he was with a lady but will not give her name. He was suspected, but the countess's lady's maid now swears her mistress was much distraught.'

'And how did you find out so much detail?'

'Well, Sir Henry, the Bow Street magistrate, is a tattletale. He confided in his wife and she told Lady Blessington and swore her to secrecy and so Lady Blessington promptly told the half of London, relieving her conscience by swearing them all to secrecy as well. Where are you going?'

'You must excuse me, Annabelle. I must go to Bow Street. You see, he was with me.'

'Matilda!'

'Not in my bed, Annabelle, but sitting, talking all night.'

'But Sir Henry has decided on suicide. If you go to him now, you will ruin your reputation and to no end.'

'You cannot stop me. This visit to London was a mistake. I shall go to Bow Street and then tomorrow I will leave for the country.'

'You are throwing away your chances of a happy life and the possibility of a good marriage for some Scotch philanderer. He could have returned home, followed her home, and put the poison in the glass.'

Matilda shook her head. 'He came straight to me. He was waiting here for me when I returned. Do not try to stop me, Annabelle. You and Emma think because you were both fortunate to find men who loved you after the deaths of *your* husbands that the same will happen to me.'

She made her way to Bow Street and waited in the magistrate's chambers. A Mr Thomas Hughes saw her enter the court. He himself had just been leaving, having been reporting on the trial of a young rip, Lord Dempster, who had been charged with breaking all the windows in Curzon Street with the butt end of his whip the night before while on a drunken spree. Mr Hughes, who wrote a column of social gossip for the *Morning Recorder*, recognized her as the widow of the late Duke of Hadshire. Scenting a scandal, he waited patiently until he saw her leave, then he sent his card in to Sir Henry.

Sir Henry was delighted to receive the reporter, for the clever Mr Hughes always referred to the magistrate in his column in flattering terms.

'I could not help noticing you received a visit from the Dowager Duchess of Hadshire,' said Mr Hughes. 'What's to go? One of her relatives in the dock?'

'Oh, dear me, nothing like that. But my lips are sealed,' said the magistrate, who had just received a blistering lecture on his gossipy ways from the forthright duchess.

'Of course they are,' said Mr Hughes, leaning back in his chair and putting his thumbs in his waistcoat. 'Ain't I always said, Sir Henry is a veritable tomb? Vastly pretty, the little duchess. Hadshire gave her a rough time, everyone knew that. Course with her money and looks, she might marry again, but said to be devilish respectable, almost a recluse. Was at that Courtneys' ball, however, the one where the late and unlamented countess dropped the cushion. Amazing how quick off the mark the print shops are! Already have pictures of the earl killing her by putting a cushion over her face. It was arsenic though, was it not?'

'Yes, and I fear the lady took her own life.'

'Thought you would have arrested the earl. That would have been a great story. Trial by his peers in the House of Lords and all that. Pity. Sure he didn't do it?'

'No, he spent the night with a lady and that lady has come forward to support his story.'

Mr Hughes leaned back farther in his chair and closed his eyes while his mind worked busily. What were the gossips saying about Torridon and that ball? That he had been obviously smitten by the widow Hadshire, and here was the widow making a call on a Bow Street magistrate. He opened his eyes and smiled slowly. 'So the little duchess was entertaining the Scottish earl all night, was she?'

'I never said that,' said Sir Henry, aghast.

'I happen to know it for a fact.'

'I am disappointed in you, Hughes,' said Sir Henry. 'I should have known you were the sort to listen at doors. Get out of here.'

'I wasn't listening at the door,' said Mr Hughes cheerfully as he got to his feet. 'But you have just answered my question.'

The following day, the Earl of Torridon settled down to make all the arrangements for his wife's burial. The body would need to be conveyed to her family home in Yorkshire. He found his butler at his elbow.

'What is it?' he snapped. 'I am not at home to any callers.'

'I know you do not read the *Morning Recorder*, my lord, but Lord Blessington's butler saw fit to bring round a copy. The social column, my lord, contains your name.'

'I have no doubt. I am not interested in the reportings of the scurrilous press.'

'Nonetheless, my lord, it does contain intelligence of which you might not be aware.'

The earl took the newspaper from him. 'While his lady was poisoning herself with arsenic, a certain Scotch lord was avisiting a certain Dowager Duchess, a visit which took all night. He and the beautiful dowager have much in common, violent death of a spouse being common to both. But his lordship's alibi is secure, for the dowager visited Bow Street to explain to the magistrate the night-time whereabouts of the noble earl.'

He threw down the paper. 'Get my carriage round,' he snapped.

He drove to Bolton Street, his only thought to see her again. But the house was locked and shuttered. A footman was emerging from the house next door and volunteered the information that the duchess had left that very morning.

The earl groaned. He could not pursue her. There was his wife's funeral to attend to. He would need to travel to Yorkshire. The fog had lifted but the day was as black and icy as his heart.

Somehow he got through the following month, dealing with his wife's parents, who held him responsible for bringing about the death of their daughter. When he returned to London, he planned to stay one day and then travel to Hadshire to see Matilda. But there was a letter from Matilda waiting for him, a letter in which she begged him never to come near her again. There was nothing he could do.

The following day he set out for Scotland, vowing never to travel south again. Although at first he could hardly bring himself to believe that his wife had committed suicide, there seemed to be no other explanation. The coroner's verdict had been 'Suicide while the state of the mind was disturbed,' and remembering her hysterical rages, he began to wonder whether she had ever been sane.

Guilt lay heavy on him. He was approaching his thirtieth year and felt he had never enjoyed any youth at all, or any laughter, or any ease.

SIX

Over a year had passed since the death of the Countess of Torridon and the scandal was largely forgotten. Emma and Annabelle still wrote to Matilda. Annabelle had given birth to a boy, Emma was expecting another, and then the letters grew less frequent as Matilda seemed determined to hide herself in the country and never emerge again.

But gradually a change was coming over Matilda as the dark events of the past receded in her mind and spring came back to England, blowing down the country lanes, sending daffodils nodding on the lawns, and bringing out shy bunches of primrose at the foot of the hedgerows.

She had gradually begun to make calls, first on some of the duke's tenants when she learned they were ill, then on some of the local gentry. Instead of leaving church on Sunday immediately after the service was over, she began to stay to talk to other members of the congregation and the vicar and his wife. Gradually she became friends with the vicar, Mr Plumtree, and his wife and family of five daughters. They were well born but did not have much money. Their house was messy and noisy and very feminine, the girls always leaving paintings or pieces of needle-work or sheets of music lying around. Matilda had vowed to herself that she would never visit London again, but she had reckoned without Letitia, the vicar's eldest daughter.

Letitia Plumtree was a giantess of a girl. She stood six feet high in her stocking soles. In an age where the average height was five feet two inches, she was regarded as something of a freak. Everything about her was big. She had large feet, thick masses of auburn hair and enormous brown eyes that looked out at the world with childlike wonder. The vicar had a rich sister who had married well and was now Lady Morton. It was expected that each daughter when she came of age would be given a Season in London, but with the callous lack of thought of needy parents, the vicar had said in front of Letitia that 'the poor girl' would not take, such was her size. The other girls would, in their turn, go to London, but Letitia's future would be to stay at home to help with the busi-ness of the parish. Matilda saw Letitia wince and her heart was touched. Letitia was also very clumsy, blundering about the small rooms of the vicarage, knocking things over.

Matilda made up her mind. She herself would give

Letitia a Season in London. She was sure it would be almost impossible to find Letitia a husband; so large a girl combined with such a small dowry stood little chance of attracting anyone in a marriage market where money was the first priority. But at least Letitia should enjoy the plays and operas, the balls and parties like her sisters.

Mr Plumtree and his wife were amazed when Matilda made her offer. They were reluctant to let her go for, clumsy as she was, Letitia was able to get through a great deal of the parish work and often wrote her father's sermons. Matilda persevered until she gained their permission.

Letitia was quite overwhelmed. She went out into the woods beyond the vicarage garden so that she could be alone with her excitement. She adored the pretty little dowager duchess. She had no hopes of finding a beau, but to go to London! To see that magical city at last!

As they eventually travelled to London, Matilda having been able to rent the same house in Bolton Street, the dowager duchess's mind turned briefly to the Earl of Torridon. Annabelle had written to say that no one had seen him in Town and he was reputed to be safe in his estates in Scotland. Matilda felt, however, that should she ever see him again, she could look upon him with equanimity. It had been a sad little episode. Fear and loneliness and distress had made her think herself in love.

The house in Bolton Street was as she remembered it. Matilda, however, became suddenly impatient of living surrounded with other people's choice of furniture. Even at the dower house, she was still surrounded with the duke's rejects. She decided that on her return to the country, she would replace everything with furniture, ornaments and paintings of her own choice.

The first week was taken up getting Letitia fitted with a new wardrobe. The first dressmaker remarked too openly on Letitia's gigantic size and was dismissed. The next was more discreet and so was engaged. Matilda privately vowed to give Letitia some lessons in deportment. The girl was apt to hunch her shoulders and walk with a stoop in an effort to reduce her height. But for the present, Matilda contented herself with taking the dazzled Letitia to all the unfashionable parts of London: the Tower, the menagerie at Exeter 'Change, the changing of the guard in Whitehall, and St Paul's Cathedral. In caring for and worrying about Letitia, she did not know her own appearance had changed. All her prettiness had come back, and her hair, once more long, rippled like a cornfield in the sun.

She sent cards to Annabelle and Emma, suggesting that for old time's sake it might be fun to meet at Mrs Trumpington's, that old lady having supplied a rendezvous for the three when their late husbands had forbidden them to meet.

She asked Letitia if she would like to remain quietly at home, but Letitia could think of no greater pleasure than meeting her patroness's best friends and said cheerfully that she would like to go.

Matilda supervised the dressing of Letitia in one of her new gowns with great care. Although her protégée could not hope to marry, there was no need for her to look other than her best. The day was chilly and so she urged Letitia to wear a rather mannish carriage dress of blue velvet with gold frogs. On her head was a rakish shako with a plume. Urged by Matilda never, ever again to stoop, Letitia, who would have done anything for her, walked with her head high.

Mrs Trumpington seemed as old and smelly and good-hearted as ever. She kissed Matilda and then stood back to look at Letitia. 'Splendid-looking gel,' she told Matilda. 'The fellows will be falling over themselves to get at her.'

'I am sure they will,' agreed Matilda, privately thinking that Mrs Trumpington was very kind.

Annabelle and Emma arrived and took an instant liking to Letitia, promising to do everything in their power to help with the girl's debut, and so the dazzled Letitia found she had not only a dowager duchess but two countesses to sponsor her.

The three old friends then fell to talking, although all Annabelle and Emma really wanted to talk about were their children: how precocious and clever, how darling, how unique!

The childless Matilda's attention began to wander. She became aware that Mrs Trumpington had a new lady's maid, a slim, sallow-faced, black-eyed female. Mrs Trumpington seemed to be very fond of her. When the maid left the room to fetch Mrs

Trumpington's shawl, the old lady said, 'That is my Clarisse. A real treasure. I do not know what I ever did without her. She reads to me and amuses me with all the gossip.'

'How long has she been with you?' asked Matilda.

'Six months. She came with an excellent reference from the Earl of Torridon.' Mrs Trumpington then looked extremely uncomfortable. 'I had forgot, Duchess, about that sad affair. So noble of you to give the earl an alibi.'

'Does Clarisse think it was suicide?' asked Matilda.

'Oh, she said there was no doubt about it. She said the poor countess only pretended to be pregnant because she was so afraid of that husband of hers and he had threatened to cast her off.'

Annabelle frowned. 'I knew Torridon's wife and, believe me, she was as tough as old boots and as vain as a peacock. She had a savage temper. Perhaps she thought she had taken enough arsenic just to give him a fright and took too much by mistake. Now *that* would be in character.'

Clarisse had entered the room while Annabelle was talking. Letitia noticed the wary look in the maid's eye and a certain stillness about her body. Letitia did not quite know why, but she took an instant dislike to the maid.

'Ah, my dear Clarisse,' said Mrs Trumpington, 'we were just talking about your late mistress. Lady Darkwood claims she was a termagant.'

'It is not my place to contradict Lady Darkwood,' said the maid.

'Loyal servant!' said Mrs Trumpington. 'Do not look so downcast, my girl. I shall give you a little present.'

How many 'little presents' had the maid had? wondered Letitia. Her gown was of silk and in quite the latest mode, and she wore a fine diamond pin in the old lace at her throat. But the duchess and her friends seemed to find nothing amiss. They have been surrounded by servants for so long, they barely notice them, thought Letitia, whereas I, with the work of the parish, am used to being on intimate terms with all ranks.

The visit was over and Letitia and Matilda left. Peter, the page, was standing on the backstrap of the carriage. He leapt down nimbly and let down the steps. And yet, mused Letitia, one could not say that the duchess ignored all servants. There were times when she treated her page more like a son than a servant.

'I am honoured to have met your friends,' said Letitia. 'But I cannot like that maid.'

'Clarisse? Well, it is nothing to do with us,' said Matilda.

'What was all that about you having supplied the Earl of Torridon with an alibi?'

'Oh, look at that quiz over there,' said Matilda. Letitia looked, but registered in her mind that the Earl of Torridon was a forbidden subject.

They were driving in an open carriage and had almost reached Bolton Street when Matilda saw Sir Charles Follett mincing along. He was pomaded and rouged and sporting a coat with padded shoulders and a padded chest. He carried his cane with an air. He saw Matilda and stopped on the wooden pavement of Piccadilly outside the blank wall that guarded Devonshire House and bowed. Then he straightened up and saw Letitia. His mouth fell open and he goggled.

Matilda coloured up with angry embarrassment for Letitia's sake.

'Who was that exquisitely dressed little man?' Letitia asked.

'A rude fop. Pay him no heed.'

Letitia sighed. The ways of London were very strange. She had thought Sir Charles looked very fine.

Ten minutes after they had entered the house, the butler appeared with a card. Matilda read it and frowned in annoyance. 'Tell Sir Charles we are not at home.'

'Why?' asked Letitia when the butler had left.

'Because he has come to gawk and gossip. The morning papers are there, Letitia. I know you like to read them. I shall leave you to them.'

Letitia loved reading newspapers. She usually kept them until late afternoon when she could have peace to browse through them without being called away to have a gown fitted and to have piano lessons, dancing lessons, or painting lessons or any of the other lessons customarily inflicted on a young lady of society who was expected to be able to show off some skill or other and to have a portfolio of watercolours to show gentleman guests.

After she had finished reading the news, she read all the social gossip. She had a good memory and liked to familiarize herself with the names of people in the ton and the gossip about them so that she would have something to talk about when she made her debut.

Then her eye fell on a malicious little item. The column so far had been an amusing one, the writer speculating on all the prizes on the marriage market and who would be most likely to snap whom up. Then the column went on, 'The Earl of T is back in London but hopeful mammas should turn their eyes elsewhere. His interest must surely lie with the Dowager Duchess of H, who supplied him with *such* a convenient alibi on the night of his wife's death.'

To her distress, Matilda found herself thinking of the Earl of Torridon constantly. At first, it was a slight, sad longing. But as the days passed, it became so intense that at times she felt haunted, as if he had taken possession of her soul.

She was grateful for all the preparations for Letitia's debut. Matilda planned to launch the girl at one of the more simple affairs. The weather had turned fine and she had an invitation to a Mr and Mrs Hammond's. It was to a breakfast, which, as was customary, would begin at three in the afternoon, no self-respecting member of the ton rising before two. It would probably be in the gardens of their house in Park Lane. There would be music and cards and some dancing. She organized an invitation for Letitia as well and then got to work on the girl's appearance. She decided that Letitia, as she could not be ignored because of her height, would have to wear something bold.

She had the added distraction of Sir Charles Follett, who kept calling, and although he was refused an audience each time, seemed blind and deaf to all the snubs. Matilda, knowing Sir Charles of old, assumed he wanted to get a preview of London's giantess so as to be ahead with the gossip as usual. Sir Charles aimed to snatch the fashionable crown from Beau Brummell, but his tailoring was too dandified and he wore too much rouge and scent. He did, however, rival the beau in one thing – dumb insolence. It had been said of Brummell when cutting someone, 'without affecting shortsightedness, he could assume that calm but wandering gaze which veers as if unconsciously round the proscribed subject, neither fixing nor to be fixed, nor occupied nor distracted'. But it was said Sir Charles cut people with much more finesse.

Sir Charles hailed from an aristocratic although untitled family. He himself had been knighted after singular bravery during the Peninsular Campaign, but it was hard now for anybody to see in the rouged fop a man who had so recently been a brave soldier.

Letitia was disappointed. She would have liked to meet this exquisite. That brief glimpse she had had of him reminded her of a favourite doll Lady Morton had sent to her for her sixth birthday. It had been a little mannikin in the more colourful dress of the last century, complete in every detail of dress down to the whalebone-stiffened skirts to his coat. The vicar had disapproved of the doll from the first, calling it a decadent plaything, and one day, when she came home from making calls with her mother, she found he had got rid of it. She had cried for days. The second reason was that Letitia was a romantic and considered there was a sad decline in the modern dress of men. A cutaway coat, originally designed for riding, was the correct morning dress, set off by that most primitive of crash helmets, the top hat, usually of beaver fur, which sat on the head without wig or powder. Skintight pantaloons that did up round the ankles, or fitted into the tops of boots, were customary. Pumps, however, were worn instead of boots in the evening. Trousers were worn only on very informal occasions. It would be so much better, thought Letitia wistfully, if men would go back to wearing paint and powder and patterned silk coats.

But the work on her own appearance soon took her mind away from Sir Charles. Matilda had chosen for her a white silk gown with a gold velvet spot. It had a low square neckline and was tied at the high waistline with a gold velvet sash. Letitia was to carry a parasol of the same material. On her head was a Lavinia straw hat ornamented round the low crown with a wreath of large artificial white silk daisies with gold velvet centres.

Matilda made her wear the whole outfit at home

for two afternoons before the breakfast so that she would be used to walking about in it.

Custom decreed that ladies must always arrive by carriage, but the day of the breakfast was so fine and warm that Matilda said there was absolutely no reason why they should not walk, Park Lane being only a short distance away. So with Peter behind them, both ladies set out. They started gaily enough but then Letitia became conscious of a change in her companion. Matilda was all at once aware of the Earl of Torridon. He was back in her mind again, haunting her, taking away all her new feeling of ease and freedom.

The Hammonds' guests were all gathered in their sunny drawing room, overlooking the garden and Hyde Park beyond. Matilda and Letitia were announced. Startled eyes regarded the giantess that was Letitia, and Matilda moved a little closer to the girl. She saw with a sinking heart that Sir Charles Follett was bearing down on them.

'Pray introduce me,' he said, gazing up in open-mouthed wonder at Letitia, all shining auburn hair and large brown eyes.

Matilda coldly introduced them and would have led Letitia away, but all at once a tall man by the window turned and faced her. It was the Earl of Torridon. Letitia noticed the way the earl turned white under his tan, the way Matilda trembled, the air that seemed to crackle with emotion and tension as he approached her. Then she heard Sir Charles say, 'Come a little away with me, Miss Plumtree, and let us leave the happy couple alone.'

'Happy couple?' demanded Letitia when they were both out of earshot.

'Well, star-crossed lovers, I think.'

'I read a really nasty piece of gossip in the *Recorder*,' said Letitia, who was every bit as forthright and candid as Matilda. 'It said the duchess gave Torridon an alibi for the night of his wife's death.'

'And so she did, and most foolish of her, for people, don't you see, began to say he had murdered his wife for the duchess. Whereas if she had left well alone, everyone would have remembered what his countess was like, apart for the fact she had shamed him disgracefully.'

Letitia smiled down at him and Sir Charles blinked and felt quite weak at the knees. It was a slow, maternal smile. He felt quite frightened and gauche and silly and at the same time desperate to impress. 'Shall we walk before the others to the garden?' he said. 'I can tell you all about it as we go.'

Totally oblivious to the startled eyes watching them, the pair walked off together.

'It was like this,' said Sir Charles. 'Our duchess was very unhappily married . . .'

'Yes, I know *that*,' said Letitia, who had heard all the local gossip about the wicked duke.

'But you see, Torridon was unhappily married as well.'

'Did you know the countess?' asked Letitia eagerly.

'Yes, quite well. Very beautiful in a cold, stately way that belied the fact that she had a rotten temper. It seemed to all and sundry that she cordially loathed her husband, but she was very possessive of him at the same time. So it seemed she was with child. I met her at the Courtneys' ball and, to my horror, she all but commanded me to dance the quadrille with her. You see, her husband had been dancing with your duchess, and they appeared enchanted with each other. I took the countess to the floor. She was leaping about like a graceful dervish, performing all those weird and wonderful ballet steps that you ladies pay a fortune to learn, when a cushion rolled out from under her gown for all to see, and, lo, we had not a pregnant – I beg your pardon – not a lady increased with a future happy event, but a slim woman minus one cushion. I near had hysterics, I can tell you. Torridon looked like the very devil. The countess ran out and reports said she went straight home and dismissed her maid and then took arsenic. Torridon had oft been heard to say he would like to kill her or wished her dead or some such stuff that is hurled about in the usual unhappy marriage, but in view of the death, it all began to seem most odd. Then the lady's maid, who had been swearing blind her mistress would not take her own life, ups and says in about the next breath that, *au contraire*, my lady was all but pulling her own hair out with mortification.'

'And where would she get the arsenic?' asked Letitia.

'Where would she . . . ? My dear and beautiful lady, *anywhere* in a London house. It is polluted with the stuff. Why, last year, I felt I was dying. Terrible mess, aches and pains and a hoarse cough. Decided if I must die, then I would do it in style. Ordered a grand bed and new hangings and chose a beautiful paper for the walls. The workmen were hovering over the paste with arsenic, and I said I didn't want any of that poisonous stuff around. New paper up. New me. I had been suffering from arsenical poisoning. It's all over the place. I became quite neurotic about it. I threw out a glass case of pretty hummingbirds because I found the creatures were full of the stuff.'

'Here come the guests,' said Letitia. 'How pale my duchess looks.'

'And behind her the earl, dark and brooding. Quite like an Elizabethan tragedy.'

'No, do not say that,' said Letitia quickly. 'She has been so gay and happy of late and we all thought she had finally recovered from her terrible marriage.'

'We must find our places at table,' he said.

'I wonder where I am sitting?' Letitia looked down the long tables in a bewildered way.

Sir Charles bowed. 'Next to me. Or I hope so, for I begged and pleaded for the honour.'

'I do not think you are a man of fashion at all,' said Letitia.

Sir Charles stiffened. 'How so?'

Again that slow, warm maternal smile. 'Because you are so very charitable, sir. You know I am a gauche country girl and much too tall and you have taken it upon yourself to be kind to me.'

'Oh, my heart,' said Sir Charles weakly.

'Are you ill?' Letitia's voice was sharp with anxiety.

'No, no. Bewildered and dumbfounded.' He raised his quizzing glass and studied the cards. 'Here we are, together as I had hoped.' He drew out a chair for her.

Letitia was relieved to notice that the earl and her duchess were seated far apart. Matilda was looking more at ease.

Sir Charles was on Letitia's right and there was an army captain on her left. The captain asked her what she thought of London, and she entertained him with a description of her visits to the Tower and all the other places no fashionable member of society would confess to having even been near.

While she talked happily, Sir Charles cast them sidelong looks. The captain was almost as tall as Letitia. What could his fair Letitia ever hope to see in a little runt like himself? He felt quite dark and miserable and small and insignificant.

But when she turned and smiled at him and began to talk to him, he could feel himself growing like a plant in the sun.

Matilda, when she found herself left alone by the gentlemen on either side of her for a few moments, studied Letitia and Sir Charles. Could she have been mistaken? Sir Charles was looking radiant and Letitia was very much at ease in his company. She had not dropped her napkin or spilled her wine or done one of the many clumsy things she usually did at table. Not only that, she seemed unaware that the very handsome captain on her other side was vainly trying to get her attention.

Her height does not matter, thought Matilda, amazed. It's all that glorious hair and those huge eyes of hers and that kind smile. Why! I may have her married after all.

But then she saw the Earl of Torridon looking at her. If only he would get out of my mind and body and thoughts and soul, thought Matilda wearily. The sun was hot and her head began to ache and she could only take comfort in the fact that her protégée was obviously enjoying herself.

After the lengthy meal was over, the guests split up into pairs and groups to promenade around the garden and admire the flowers.

Letitia had been swept off by the captain, much to her disappointment. She eventually excused herself and went in search of Matilda.

She saw the top of the Earl of Torridon's head. He was standing in a far corner of the garden, behind a stand of bushes, talking earnestly to someone, and Letitia felt sure that someone was Matilda. The earl seemed angry and Letitia walked forward to rescue the duchess.

But the sound of Matilda's voice stopped her short. 'I cannot marry you,' she was saying. 'I cannot believe your wife killed herself.'

'Are you trying to say that *I* killed her?' The earl sounded at the end of his tether. Letitia stayed where she was, listening.

'No, but someone did,' said Matilda. 'If only the mystery of her death were cleared up, I would feel not so guilty and sad and worried.'

'I have tried to forget you,' said the earl, 'but I found I could not. You are constantly in my thoughts, Matilda. I *yearn* for you.'

Letitia drew back, suddenly embarrassed. She almost collided with Sir Charles. 'There you are, fair lady,' he said cheerfully.

'Oh, come with me,' cried Letitia. 'I need your help.'

Happy but bewildered, Sir Charles trotted after her, trying to keep up with her long strides.

'Good, the guests are starting to go indoors,' said Letitia. 'What I have to say to you is private.'

'And what is that, my heart of hearts?' said Sir Charles, but Letitia was too worried to notice the endearment.

'We simply must find out who killed the Countess of Torridon.'

'Sir Charles blinked up at her in the sunlight. 'We?' he asked faintly.

'I cannot do such a thing myself,' said Letitia. 'But you are a man of fashion, and intelligent and kind.' She smiled at him suddenly, and he blushed with happiness under his rouge. All in that moment, he would have done anything for her. Sir Charles had a large and domineering mother and was usually apt to find himself pulled helplessly into the orbit of large and domineering women. But never before had he been so smitten, and with one who was obviously pure and good-hearted. She made him feel like one of the knights of the Round Table.

'Tish,' he said, airily waving a scented

handkerchief. 'Should be no great matter. But why is it so important?'

'He, the earl, wishes to marry my duchess, and she him, but she says she cannot while his wife's death remains a mystery.'

'Could she not,' said Sir Charles, cautiously and suddenly aware of the magnitude of the task she was about to set him, 'just go ahead and marry him? Oh, I know there was that piece of tittle-tattle in the newspapers. But society has such a short memory,' he added hopefully.

'But it is what *she* feels that matters,' said Letitia. 'I know where we could start.'

'Where?' asked Sir Charles, feeling relieved, for he could not possibly think of any plan of action.

'Her maid. The Countess of Torridon's maid is now working for a certain Mrs Trumpington. We could call on Mrs Trumpington and ask her if we might speak to her maid!'

'But how are we to effect that?' asked Sir Charles. 'I have called at Bolton Street on innumerable occasions to see you and the dowager duchess would not admit me.'

'Perhaps she thought you were amusing yourself. Whereas I now know you are a very kind and elegant gentleman who is indulging a silly girl.'

'Not at all,' he protested, but that word 'girl' gave him pause. He was thirty-two, a great age, and she was surely only about seventeen or eighteen. He felt old and withered. It was obvious she looked on him as a sort of father.

'I will speak to the duchess,' he said after a little pause, 'and arrange to take you driving tomorrow. Tell her we are going to call on Mrs Trumpington briefly for you have taken a fondness for the old horro . . . old lady.'

'Oh, thank you,' breathed Letitia.

'I think your chaperone is still out in the shrubbery. We should go indoors and have a cool glass of champagne and talk further.'

'I should go to see what Letitia is doing,' Matilda was saying.

'That tall Amazon? I should say Sir Charles is minding her very carefully,' replied the earl.

'That is what upsets me. Sir Charles is such a fribble. He cannot really be interested in a green girl. She is so young and fresh and he is comparatively old and painted and primped.'

'He has a good heart, I believe. And talking of hearts . . .'

Matilda held up a little hand. 'No, we will not talk of hearts. Let us talk of something else. We could be friends.'

'Dearest duchess, I have many friends, but I do not burn and ache to hold them in my arms.'

Matilda looked at him sadly. 'You are incorrigible, sir.'

He looked around quickly and then jerked her roughly into his arms. From far away came the chatter of the voices of the guests and the jaunty strains of a country dance. 'Oh, Matilda,' he said with a break in his voice. He bent his head and kissed her, not the hard, punishing kiss she had been expecting, but firm and gentle and warm. But she moved in his embrace and he could feel her breasts pressed against him. He held her even more tightly and buried his mouth in her own until she let out a muffled groan of passion. She had once seen a dry gorse bush set on fire, and it had burned up with a white-hot flame. That, thought Matilda dizzily, was what was happening to her body. He freed her lips at last and said huskily, 'I could get a special licence. We could be married quietly.'

She gave him a drowned look. 'I will keep you in this garden and kiss you and kiss you until you say yes,' he whispered. 'Think of it. No one need know, not for a little. We could go away together, be together.' His mouth caressed hers and one hand stroked her breast. 'All night long, my love.'

Matilda's experience of the marriage bed had been nasty, to say the least. And yet he was stroking her breast and she was powerless to stop him. Instead her body craved more intimacies. The sun was hot, beating down on them, putting into both fevered minds thoughts of cool flesh against cool flesh in some darkened bedchamber.

'Let me think,' said Matilda urgently. 'I cannot think clearly when you hold me.'

He released her but took her hand in his. 'The only way we can ever think clearly is when we can burn some of this frustrated passion away, and yet you must be my wife. I cannot take you, else.'

'Now you see,' whispered Letitia as the couple walked in from the garden, 'why we must do something quickly. They are so very much in love.'

Sir Charles thought in a bewildered way that only a short time ago he would have been maliciously titillated by the earl and dowager duchess and would probably have made up a poem about them to amuse society. Now he was so dazed, so happy, he wished all the world well.

Matilda was wrenched between happiness and worry. The effect Torridon had on her body and mind was frightening her. If she married him, news of that marriage would leak out sooner or later, and then gossips would say it was proof the earl had murdered his late wife. Then Mrs Hammond swept up, demanding that the earl dance with one of the wallflowers, and Matilda found Sir Charles at her elbow.

'I crave your leave to take Miss Plumtree driving on the morrow,' he said.

Matilda studied him. 'I will be direct,' she said in her rather deep voice, and Sir Charles groaned inwardly. 'Miss Plumtree is but turned eighteen and unaccustomed to the ways of the world. She is a trifle large for a lady and I do not wish her to be the butt of one of your silly jokes or poems. Do I make myself clear?'

'Since frank talking appears to be the order of the day,' said Sir Charles, 'I shall state my intentions bluntly. I wish your permission to pay my addresses to Miss Plumtree.'

'Good heavens!' Matilda was startled. 'I do not know what to say, Sir Charles.'

'Try saying yes,' he remarked waspishly.

'It is all very sudden, sir.' Matilda frowned. 'I will not discourage you from seeing her, but I beg you to get to know each other a little better before declaring yourself.' She looked at him curiously. 'Does Mrs Follett know of your marriage plans?' Everyone knew of Sir Charles's battle-axe of a mother. She lived in a villa in Hampstead but occasionally came to Town and could be seen looming behind her son like a grim wardress.

A cloud crossed Sir Charles's eyes. But then he said, 'Miss Plumtree appears to have conceived a fondness for Mrs Trumpington and wishes to call on her tomorrow. My mother will be in residence at Bright's Hotel. With your permission, I would like to take Miss Plumtree to meet her.'

'By all means,' said Matilda, her face clearing. The matter was solved. Mrs Follett would soon put to rout any ideas her son might have of marriage, and at least it would do Letitia's reputation no harm to be seen being courted by one of London's gilded butterflies.

'I will grant you two hours tomorrow afternoon,' said Matilda. 'We go to Vauxhall in the evening. Make sure Letitia is home by five o'clock.'

Sir Charles made an elaborate bow and backed away with many flourishes of a scented handkerchief as if retreating before royalty.

Matilda felt she should now turn her mind to her own problems. She had surely disgraced herself enough for one day. She had been painfully aware of all eyes turned in their direction when she had walked into the room with the earl. She would ignore him for the rest of the day and make up her mind what to do when she was back at home and had peace to examine her thoughts. He was dancing with quite a pretty girl. When he smiled down at her, Matilda suddenly felt torn with jealousy. Of what use were her scruples if it meant he was going to be snatched up by some female who did not give a rap?

The following dance was a waltz, but before the earl could reach her, her hand was claimed by the captain who had sat next to Letitia at dinner. His name was Captain Emsley and it turned out his sole purpose in soliciting the duchess to dance was to talk about Letitia. 'I feel it my duty to point out, ma'am,' he said, 'that Miss Plumtree should be warned against Sir Charles. We all know he has nothing in his head other than the designs for a new embroidered waist-coat, and yet he is monopolizing Miss Plumtree. I wanted her to go driving with me tomorrow and Miss Plumtree told me she was already engaged to go driving with Sir Charles!'

'Yes, Sir Charles did ask my permission,' said Matilda.

The captain trod angrily on her foot. 'It ought to be stopped,' he muttered.

'If I find the prospect of a drive displeases Letitia, then I shall tell Sir Charles she cannot go. I really cannot do anything further,' said Matilda, feeling it was all very aging being treated like the girl's mother.

'I've a good mind to call him out,' said the captain

angrily, and trod on the hem of her gown this time. There was a ripping sound and Matilda exclaimed in dismay.

'You have torn my gown, Captain,' she said, 'and now you must excuse me while I effect some repairs.'

Stammering and blushing miserably, the captain made his apologies.

Matilda approached Mrs Hammond and explained her predicament. Mrs Hammond led her to a small morning room and said she would send a maid along but Matilda protested. She was well able to mend a tear in a gown. A needle and thread would suffice. So Mrs Hammond found her a work basket and left her to it.

Matilda sat down on a small sofa covered in gold satin and began to stitch at the rip in one of the flounces of her gown.

The door opened and the earl walked in. She stayed frozen, looking at him, the needle poised in one hand. He knelt at her feet and, with a little sigh, buried his head in her lap.

She put down the needle and thread and stroked his thick black hair with a trembling hand. They stayed like that for a long time, only dimly aware of the far-off music and of the birds singing in the twilight of the garden outside. The window of the morning room was open and the heavy scent of lilac from a tree laden with purple blossoms just outside the window crept into the room.

Letitia quietly opened the door. She had been searching for Matilda. She stood transfixed. Matilda raised her eyes and saw her, but she did not move. Letitia went out and quietly closed the door.

Sir Charles met her as she was making her way back to the long room where the dancing was being held. He noticed tears in her large pansy-brown eyes and he caught her hand.

'What is it?' he asked quickly. 'What has happened?'

'I think we must find out who murdered the Countess of Torridon and very quickly,' said Letitia.

Sir Charles's eyes were suddenly shrewd but kind. He fished in his pocket and handed her a large handkerchief edged in priceless lace. Letitia gave her nose a hearty blow and gave him a dizzying smile, saying she would have it laundered.

'Keep it,' he said, looking up at her. 'Perhaps it will remind you of me.'

'Oh, I do not need anything to make me do that,' said Letitia. Sir Charles executed a funny sort of hop, skip and jump out of pure happiness before collecting himself and offering her his arm and leading her back to the party.

SEVEN

Matilda had made no arrangements to meet the earl. She was bewildered and shaken and could only manage a weak smile in Letitia's direction as that young lady cheerfully went off the following afternoon with Sir Charles.

Annabelle and Emma called as soon as she had left. Nothing in Matilda's manner betrayed her inner turmoil, but Emma and Annabelle were amazed at the change in their friend's appearance. The dowager duchess had not only regained all her former beauty, but there was a new softness and a glow about her. Emma and Annabelle exchanged glances. Matilda must be in love. They plied her with questions about what she had been doing and whom she had seen, and Matilda replied with seeming placidity and not once mentioned the Earl of Torridon's name.

Letitia and Sir Charles found to their alarm that

Mrs Trumpington was ill and could not receive visitors. Sir Charles was about to turn away, but Letitia said airily, 'Then we should see her. It is bad for invalids to lie isolated from their friends.'

The butler looked at her nervously, but the orders that madam was not to be disturbed came from Clarisse and the butler loathed Clarisse. Clarisse had begun to assume all the airs of mistress of the house, and as Mrs Trumpington doted on the maid, her other servants were afraid that the old lady was about to die and leave everything to Clarisse.

'I will take you to her,' he said, making up his mind.

Mrs Trumpington was lying in a great four-poster bed in a darkened room. She looked as small as a child.

Clarisse appeared from a corner of the room and tried to shoo Letitia and Sir Charles away, but Mrs Trumpington said feebly, 'Who is it?'

'It is I, Mrs Trumpington,' said Letitia. 'Miss Plumtree. What ails you?'

'I do not know,' said the old lady. 'I had an attack of vomiting, my bones ache and my throat is devilish sore.'

'Let us have some light in here,' said Sir Charles in a strained voice, unlike his usual light tones. Ignoring the maid's cry that light would hurt her mistress's eyes, Sir Charles pulled back the curtains and then opened the windows. Sunlight and fresh air flooded into the room.

'Beg pardon, ma'am,' said Sir Charles earnestly,

'but I cannot help comparing your symptoms to those I once suffered. Any arsenic in the house?'

Clarisse stood very still. Outside a hawker cried, 'Sand Ho!' in a raucous voice.

'Why?' asked Mrs Trumpington faintly.

'Well, demme, if I hadn't the same thing and it was poisoning from arsenic in the paper in my bedchamber.'

'But the walls are painted.'

'Must be somewhere. I have a horror of the stuff.'

'There is no arsenic in this house,' said Clarisse harshly.

'Better make sure. Stay and talk to madam, Miss Plumtree. Hate arsenic. I'll see that butler fellow and get him to make a search.'

Clarisse made a move to follow him, but Mrs Trumpington said in a weak voice, 'Do raise me a little, Clarisse, so that I may see Miss Plumtree.'

Sir Charles followed the butler down to the kitchens. The cook and housekeeper said there was arsenic, of course there was. Kept down the rats and black beetles, it did. Sir Charles cheerfully commandeered all of it and said they were not to allow any in the house. Then he turned to the butler. 'I must ask you to show me the servants' sleeping quarters. The maids in particular will take the stuff, perhaps, to clear their complexions.'

The butler saw nothing odd in this. He was old and used to a lifetime of coping with the eccentric ways of the quality. Sir Charles gave a perfunctory look around the female servants' quarters and then asked casually to see Clarisse's room. 'Don't disturb anything,' said the butler. 'Very high and mighty is our lady's maid and already hinting the old lady is going to leave her everything in her will.'

Sir Charles carefully searched Clarisse's room. He was amazed at the richness of her gowns and the quantity of her jewellery. 'Nothing,' he muttered. 'Now, where I wonder . . . ?' He walked over to the toilet table. 'Ah, here it is. Innocent as anything. In a little apothecary's box for all to see. I'll have that as well.'

He returned to Mrs Trumpington's bedchamber and spilled all his finds on the bed. 'You were wrong,' he said to Clarisse. 'The place is *stuffed* with arsenic, and I even found some in your own room.'

'You had no right!' exclaimed Clarisse, her hands clenched.

'He means well,' said Mrs Trumpington mildly. 'Why are you so agitated, my girl?'

'I feel so silly,' said Clarisse. 'I use a little to keep my complexion clear and fine. It is embarrassing to be caught out in such a petty piece of vanity.'

'There, there, do not distress yourself,' said Mrs Trumpington. 'I think your theory is very far-fetched, Sir Charles. There are so many fevers and agues in London and I am very old.'

'And so you are, very,' said Sir Charles. 'But you can never be too careful at your age. Stomach gets very delicate. Tell you what, before you taste anything, get Clarisse to taste it first. Seems devoted to you. Sure you'd be glad to do it, hey, Clarisse?'

'Of course,' said Clarisse in a colourless voice.

Letitia bent forward and kissed Mrs Trumpington on that lady's withered cheek. 'We will call to see you very soon,' she said softly.

Outside the house, Letitia faced Sir Charles, who was holding packets of arsenic. 'You all but accused that maid of trying to poison her mistress.'

Sir Charles shrugged. 'If she ain't, she's got a clear conscience; if she is, then we've put a spoke in her wheel. Don't like that Clarisse. French, my hatband. That's the trouble with all you ladies demanding French maids. The Claras of this world promptly change their names to Clarisse, or Yvette, or Françoise, or something, and then their mistresses marvel at their command of the English language. Mind you, she's got a good incentive to get rid of the old lady if Mrs Trumpington plans to leave her anything. Butler said Clarisse was hinting she expects to inherit everything. But why the Countess of Torridon? We'll call soon and keep the pot boiling. Now to see my mother. I sent a note around earlier warning her to expect us.'

Mrs Follett was a large, muscular woman with an orange moustache, orange because she bleached the hairs of her upper lip. She had a massive bosom and several chins. She was not alarmed by the proposed call on her by this Miss Plumtree. She had routed a few females that her son seemed keen on before and with little difficulty. She was looking forward to the battle to come.

134

Sir Charles and Letitia were ushered into Mrs Follett's private hotel sitting room. Mrs Follett looked up at Letitia and felt her spirits sink. She had never felt as dwarfed in her life before as she did now. Sir Charles made the introductions. Mrs Follett rang the bell and ordered tea. Sir Charles, looking increasingly uneasy, said he would like something stronger and was told in no uncertain terms to sit down and behave himself.

Letitia studied Mrs Follett with wide-eyed interest. She was exactly like old Mrs Browning in the village. Mrs Browning had domineered her only son for ages, but he had finally left her and married a girl half his age. Letitia had called on Mrs Browning shortly after the wedding and found that unlovely woman quite devastated. Her son had been her whole life.

Mrs Follett questioned Letitia closely about her family, her relations, how she came to meet the dowager duchess, more like an interrogator at a tribunal than a hostess.

Sir Charles sat miserably in a chair. It was going to happen again. Mother would ask him to go for a walk so that she could get to know Miss Plumtree better and he would go for that walk and come back to find a flushed and embarrassed Letitia, a Letitia who did not want to have anything more to do with him.

He made up his mind to stay. But when his mother told him to go for a walk, he found the protest dying on his lips. She would throw a temper tantrum if he did not. He knew that of old. 'Damme,' he muttered, and he strolled along Bond Street, 'if Torridon did murder his missus, then good luck to him. A nagging, shouting female is the very devil.'

'So am I to understand,' Mrs Follett was saying sweetly, 'that you have very little dowry?'

Letitia smiled. 'I have not been so vulgar as to ask the amount for, as you know, Mrs Follett, no *lady* would dare to ask so vulgar a question. But we are as poor as church mice, I do assure you.'

Mrs Follett's orange moustache bristled. 'But one must always discuss money when marriage is proposed, and since my boy has no father . . .'

She broke off. Letitia was glowing with happiness. 'Marriage!' she breathed, clasping her hands.

Seriously alarmed, Mrs Follett exclaimed, 'You go too fast. Nothing was said of marriage.'

'Ah, I see,' said Letitia comfortably. 'It is your normal practice to ask visitors about their finances.'

'Yes. No!' shouted Mrs Follett. She pulled herself together with an effort and tried another tack. She forced a laugh. 'Of course I know you are not thinking of marriage, that my Charles cannot be thinking of marriage.'

Letitia leaned forward and squeezed one of Mrs Follett's pudgy hands. Her large eyes brimmed with sympathetic tears. 'You poor, dear lady,' she said.

Mrs Follett snatched her hand away. 'What *can* you mean?'

'You are just like Mrs Browning,' sighed Letitia. 'Poor woman. Her son was all in all to her. She kept him close and kept the ladies at bay. But he eventually married a very strong-willed lady and refused to see his mother again. She, poor thing, was left desperately lonely for she had made no friends, her son being everything to her. She did not know how to make friends, having not ever been in the way of it, and so everyone shunned her. What a lonely, miserable old age. It quite breaks my heart to think of it.'

Letitia was only being honest, but Mrs Follett began to feel very weak and frightened. She thought that Letitia was threatening her, that Letitia was saying that she was that same type of strong-willed lady who would snatch Charles away and that Charles would never be allowed to come near his mother again.

'You will marry my son over my dead body!' she shouted.

'Never say that,' cried Letitia. 'I am sure you have years and years to live yet and will dance at his wedding. I am glad we were able to talk so freely, Mrs Follett, for I had been quite prepared to meet a battle-axe, for as you know, that is what cruel society does call you. But what do I find? A charming but lonely lady who is terrified of facing more loneliness.'

Rage nearly choked Mrs Follett. But her son entered the room having decided he could not stay away a moment longer, and her anger died away as she looked at him in a pleading way that he had never seen before.

'I am tired and must lie down, Charles.'

'I shall leave you.' Letitia got to her feet and then stooped and kissed Mrs Follett on the cheek. 'But never fear, I shall be back to see you very soon.'

Sir Charles heard his mother utter something very like a whimper as he led Letitia out.

He kept staring up at Letitia in a worried way. She smiled down at him and said, 'Your mama will be all right when she has had a rest. I am convinced she is really very strong.'

'As strong as a horse,' said Sir Charles bitterly.

'But very lonely. I think we should call on her as much as possible while she is in Town.'

'You mean you actually want to see her again?'

'Of course. She is your mother, after all.'

Sir Charles grinned. 'Well, if that don't beat all,' he said sunnily. 'Tell you what, I'll take you home and then I'll go back to Mrs Trumpington and tell her if she's made any stupid sort of will to make another sensible one and tell everyone about it, including Clarisse, if you get my meaning.'

'Do be careful,' warned Letitia.

'Oh, I shall. I won't take a bite to eat or a sup to drink in that house.'

'And I had better go and get prettified for Vauxhall.'

'Waste of time,' said Sir Charles, driving expertly along Bond Street. 'You are pretty enough already.'

Letitia glowed like a sunrise. 'You are the very best of men,' she said.

'I am?' Sir Charles reined in his horses and looked up at her in bewildered delight. For a long moment they stared at each other until several harsh voices from other drivers told them to move along.

* * *

Mrs Trumpington was surprised and amused to receive yet another visit from the frivolous Sir Charles. But her amusement faded as Sir Charles dismissed Clarisse, checked the door to make sure the maid was not listening, and then hitched his chair close to the bed.

'Have you made a will, ma'am?' he asked.

'As a matter of fact I have,' snapped Mrs Trumpington. 'What's it to you?'

'Tell you in a minute. Who've you left everything to? Go on. It's a matter of life and death. Your death, I mean.'

'You are an impertinent jackanapes. Well, since you must know, I have left everything to my dear Clarisse.'

'Look here,' said Sir Charles urgently, 'your so dear Clarisse was maid to the Countess of Torridon. She died of arsenical poisoning. You say you are going to leave everything to Clarisse and now I find you yourself, ma'am, suffering what looks like arsenical poisoning. Clarisse had arsenic in her room.'

'I will never believe such a thing of that girl. Never!'

'Say she's innocent. Then to make sure, all you have to do is cancel your will. You can write it again in a few months. Who did you leave it to originally?'

'My grandson. But I have not seen him this age.'

'What's his name?'

'Mr Jeffrey Trumpington.'

'Wait a bit.' Sir Charles rang the bell. Clarisse promptly appeared. 'I want to see the butler,' said

Sir Charles, 'and make yourself scarce until I have finished my call.'

'You must humour him, Clarisse,' said Mrs Trumpington, giving the maid an indulgent smile.

Clarisse bobbed a curtsy, threw a venomous look, quickly veiled, in Sir Charles's direction, and left the room.

The butler appeared and Sir Charles asked him, 'Are you sure Mr Jeffrey Trumpington has not been to call?'

The butler's reply startled Mrs Trumpington. 'But he has been to call, several times, but I had instructions to tell him Mrs Trumpington was not at home to him.'

'I gave no such instructions,' said Mrs Trumpington.

'Clarisse told all the servants that you never wanted to see him again and as you are so close to your maid, madam, we could not do aught but believe her.'

'You may go,' said the old lady faintly. 'You, too, Sir Charles. I am much indebted to you. I would rather handle this myself.'

'You are in danger,' said Sir Charles bluntly.

Mrs Trumpington gave a thin smile. 'When you get to my great age, young man, death does not hold the same fears. Get you gone and send that maid to me.'

Mrs Trumpington pulled herself up on her pillows after Sir Charles had left. She fished in a drawer of her bedside table and pulled out a small pistol and bullets and carefully loaded it. Then she tugged on the bell rope. Clarisse appeared and stood at the end of the bed.

'I have just learned that you have been turning away my own grandson at the door. I made a will in your favour, Clarisse, and you manipulated a lonely old woman into doing it. As to the reasons for my ill health and the late Countess of Torridon's death, I shudder to think. My lawyer will call here tomorrow afternoon and I will rectify a great wrong.' She placed the loaded pistol pointedly in front of her on the bed.

Clarisse began to cry and through her sobs she said she was innocent of wishing her mistress any harm. As to turning away Mr Jeffrey, she, Clarisse, thought that Mr Jeffrey was only interested in her mistress's money and should be discouraged. She was innocent of all else, she swore. What would become of her now? Without a reference, she would die in the workhouse.

She seemed so overwrought and at the same time so sincere that Mrs Trumpington almost found herself believing the maid. She was an old lady and prey to many ills. It could not be poison. But it was a risk she was frightened to take.

In a softer voice, she said, 'You may stay until the end of the month and I shall give you a good reference, but you must stay no longer than that!'

Matilda had invited Captain Emsley to their box at Vauxhall. But to her surprise, Letitia did not seem at all dazzled by the lights and music and spectacles of the famous pleasure gardens. Nor did she seem particularly interested in the captain. She appeared to listen to him with half an ear while scanning the crowds. I do believe she is looking for that popinjay, Sir Charles, thought Matilda. Then her own thoughts turned as usual to the Earl of Torridon. Why had he not called? She, too, began to scan the crowds, and the captain ended up sitting between them in a moody silence.

'Why, there is Sir Charles!' exclaimed Letitia, suddenly lighting up. Sir Charles approached their box quickly. He was not his usual urbane self, but asked if he might have permission to take Letitia for a stroll. The captain looked ready to explode so Letitia, without waiting for Matilda's answer, said, 'Of course.'

When they had left, Matilda gave the captain a rueful smile. 'I am afraid that my charge is much taken with Sir Charles. I fail to understand why.'

'Man-milliner,' said the captain sulkily. 'I was to be her escort for this evening, and it would have been good manners to treat me to some common civility. There is nothing more lowering than to be sitting with a lady whose thoughts are on something else. I said,' he repeated, his voice rising, '*there is nothing more lowering than to be sitting with a lady whose thoughts are on someone else.*' But Matilda had seen the Earl of Torridon in the crowd and was waving to him. The earl did not trouble to mount to the box by the steps at the back but vaulted over the front.

'Walk with me,' he said abruptly to Matilda. 'I must be private with you.'

The captain watched them go. Then he pulled forward the bowl of rack punch for which the gardens were famous and proceeded to get thoroughly drunk.

'I think we should tell the duchess of this immediately,' cried Letitia after she had heard Sir Charles's story.

Sir Charles wished now he had left the tale of his adventures at Mrs Trumpington's until later in the evening. They were promenading along one of the garden's dark walks. This was the evening when he had planned to kiss her. He had been tempted to carry a box with him so that he could stand on it to reach her lips. But he thought that would make him look foolish and so planned to lead her into a quiet grove where the plinth of a statue might be able to raise him to the required height.

But she looked so worried and anxious that he knew he would need to put off romance until later.

They returned to the box. When they entered it to ask the captain the whereabouts of Matilda, he staggered to his feet, raised his fists, and advanced on Sir Charles. 'I am going to give you the thrashing you deserve,' shouted the captain. Sir Charles moved to the balcony of the box and stood with his back to it, facing the captain. With a roar like an enraged bull, Captain Emsley rushed headlong at him, his fists swinging. Sir Charles stepped neatly aside and the captain crashed into the flimsy balcony, which broke. He landed in among the laughing crowd below.

'I'll wager she's gone off with Torridon,' said Sir

Charles. 'What else would make her abandon her guest? Let us go and search for her before that oafish captain recovers.'

'I don't know where to begin to look,' said Letitia as they walked away from the supper boxes.

'But I do,' said Sir Charles. 'I know every pesky grove in this place where lovers might lurk.' He coloured and then added quickly, 'I have such reprehensible friends.'

In one of the darkest of the groves, the earl and Matilda sat side by side on a rustic bench.

'You have been silent long enough,' said the earl. 'What is your answer? I have the special licence. We can be married in two weeks' time.'

'We would be crucified by the gossips,' said Matilda. 'I am such a coward. I would rather be your mistress.'

'And make the scandal worse? Are you going to let two horrible people, your late husband and my late wife, ruin our happiness?' He put his hands on her shoulders and turned her to face him. His hands slid up to the smoothness of her neck and his long fingers caressed the white skin. 'You are trembling, Matilda,' he murmured. 'Kiss me!'

'We cannot interrupt them!' whispered Letitia as she and Sir Charles finally discovered the couple. 'Come away!'

But Sir Charles thought that he had put aside kisses himself that evening and all for the sake of this wretched couple. Ignoring Letitia, he said loudly, 'Ahem!'

Matilda and the earl broke apart.

'How dare you . . . ?' began the earl wrathfully, but Sir Charles held up his hand. Succinctly he outlined the events of the day.

'Clarisse,' said the earl slowly. 'Of course. But why?'

Sir Charles shook his head. 'I can think of no reason.'

'I think you have saved Mrs Trumpington's life,' said Matilda. 'Why did you not tell me of your suspicions before, Letitia?'

'I overheard you at the Hammonds' saying you could not marry until you found out who murdered the countess,' said Letitia, 'and Sir Charles here said he would help me. We decided to start with Clarisse.'

'Proving she was trying to poison Mrs Trumpington is one thing,' said the earl. 'Proving she poisoned my wife is another.'

'Oh, Sir Charles will think of something,' declared Letitia blithely. 'So you may as well get married.'

'That is something only we can decide.' Matilda stood up. 'The hour is late, Letitia. It is time we went home.'

Letitia walked back toward the bright lights on Sir Charles's arm, feeling very disappointed.

When she was alone in the carriage with Matilda, she said, 'Why could we not stay? It is not late and you could have spent more time with your earl.'

'I have much to think about,' replied Matilda, turning her face away. For how could she tell this virgin that she could not trust herself alone with the earl?

She had not answered his question. She dreaded the scandal. But how could she live without him?

Letitia heaved a great sigh.

'I am sorry,' said Matilda quickly. 'I fear I ruined your evening. Do you like Sir Charles very much?'

'He is the most wonderful man in the world.'

'But, my dear, he is much older than you. You have not really had a chance to meet other men.' Matilda wondered whether to tell Letitia that Sir Charles wanted to marry her, but decided against it. Surely Letitia would be happier with someone of her own age.

Letitia sighed again. 'We shall do something tomorrow to raise your spirits,' said Matilda. 'We will go at some unfashionably early hour to the mercers on Ludgate Hill and choose a dress.' Choosing a dress meant buying material for one.

'And may I see Sir Charles later?' Letitia looked stubborn.

'Very well. But do promise me that you will make a push to get to know some other gentlemen.'

Letitia frowned. 'If I pointed out to you, Duchess, that you were likely to cause a great scandal by marrying the Earl of Torridon and that you really ought to look elsewhere, what would your answer be?'

'That is not the same thing! I am older than you and more used to the ways of the world. Now we will rise early and go to Ludgate Hill. We have both been invited to a ball at Devonshire House. Very grand. You must have something dazzling to wear and so must I.'

Some of the finest mercers shops were on Ludgate Hill, including among their wares Dutch rateens, duffles, friezes, beaver coating, kerseymeres, German serges, Wilton stuffs, sagathies, nankeen, Silesia cambrics, Manchester velvets, silks, grosgrams, allapeens, double allapeens, silk camblets, barragins, Brussels camblets, princes stuffs, worsted damasks, silk knitpieces, corded silks, gattias, shagg velvets, serge desoys and shalloons.

The shops were like gilded theatres and the mercers, the performers. They were very effeminate gentlemen: the 'sweetest, fairest, nicest, dished-out creatures', as one Regency observer described it.

As Matilda and Letitia looked in at these shop doors, the mercers would cry out, 'Garden silks, ladies' Italian silks, very fine mantua silks, and right Geneva velvet, English velvet, velvet embossed?' Or at the doorway of one of the meaner shops came the call, 'Fine thread satins, both stripe and plain, fine mohair silks, satinets, burdets, Perianets, Norwich crapes, anterines, silks for hoods and scarves, hair camlets, druggets, sagathies, gentlemen's nightgowns ready-made, shalloons, durances and right Scotch plaids.'

Letitia, following Matilda into one of these shops, was amused by the blandishments of the mercers of whom there were three: one to flatter, one to produce the material, and the other to stand by the door and hand the customers in and out of their carriages. One mercer skipped up and then executed so low a bow that his nose nearly touched the sanded floor. Then he leapt back a pace and clasped his hands in delight as he regarded Matilda. He snapped his fingers and another mercer ran up with a bolt of blue silk, which he unravelled and cast round the shoulders of the first mercer. Then the sales talk started in earnest. 'This, madam, is wonderful charming. This, madam, is so diverting a silk. This madam, my stars! How cool it looks! But this, madam, ye gods! Would I had ten thousand yards of it!' He then fashioned some of the blue silk into a sleeve and held it up against Matilda's shoulder. 'It suits Your Grace's face wonderful well.' Your Grace, because the man at the door had interpreted the coat of arms on Matilda's carriage and signalled her importance in a sort of dumb show.

'I shall pay you ten shillings a yard for it,' said Matilda at last, after the mercer had demanded fifteen.

The mercer leapt back a step. 'Fan me ye winds!' he cried. 'Your Grace rallies me. Should I part with it at such a price, the weavers would rise upon the very shop. Was you at the Park last night, madam? Your Grace shall have this precious silk reduced by sixpence. Have you read *The Tatler* today?' And so he rattled on while Matilda, used to bargaining, finally managed to get it for twelve shillings a yard.

Letitia was content to stand and watch the activity around her. The mercer swirled bolts of cloth about the shop, trying to persuade Matilda to buy more. 'I have bought enough for myself,' said Matilda firmly. 'I now wish a gown for my young friend here.'

The mercer's little mouth opened in surprise as he took in Letitia's great height, then he sighed in ecstasy and called to the other two in a high, breathless voice, 'Your help, sirs. Silk for miss.'

The three performed a sort of ballet around Letitia, each marvelling at the glorious amount of silk it would take to cover such a height.

'Your first lesson in shopping.' Matilda laughed. 'I am going next door to buy ribbons, Letitia. Choose the colour of silk that you think suits you best, fix a price, and I shall pay for it when I return.'

Letitia nodded. Silks swirled around her tall form and then, as if through the parting of curtains in the theatre, she saw the shifting crowd in the street outside, and there among that crowd, hurrying along with her head bent, scurried Clarisse.

She gave a stifled exclamation, twirled around to free herself from a swathe of golden silk, called out, 'I shall take it', and ran from the shop.

An exasperated duchess found on her return that her protégée had purchased a vast amount of gold-coloured silk at fifteen shillings a yard and had run out of the shop. She went out herself. But among the shifting crowds of Ludgate Hill, there was no sign of Letitia. Matilda settled down to wait her return, for surely she would come back and explain what had sent her off at a run.

Glad for once of her extra height, Letitia was able to keep Clarisse in view without walking too close behind her. Up Ludgate Hill went the maid, along Ludgate Street, and then, just before St Paul's Cathedral, she turned right down Creed Lane. Letitia turned the corner just in time to see Clarisse enter an apothecary's shop.

Was she going to buy arsenic? Letitia walked closer to the shop. After a very short time Clarisse emerged. Letitia drew back into a doorway as the maid scurried past, her head down. Letitia watched as Clarisse gained the corner of the street and hailed a hack.

She walked into the apothecary's shop. A tiny man stood behind the counter. 'I wonder, was my maid here a moment ago?' asked Letitia.

'There was a lady just here but too finely dressed for a maid.'

'Brown satin with a lace collar and a pelisse of the same material and a close bonnet?' asked Letitia breathlessly.

'Yes, I have just served her.'

'And did she buy that arsenic powder for the rats?'

'Oh, yes, madam.'

'Good,' said Letitia faintly.

She rushed out of the shop and tried to hurry along the street and down Ludgate Hill. The crowd was so dense and the road so thick with traffic, she thought she would never get back to Matilda.

Matilda was haggling over Letitia's purchase of gold silk. At last the mercer, who had enjoyed the battle, conceded defeat and set the price at thirteen shillings a yard, but still insisted Letitia wanted all of it. Matilda was just gloomily reflecting that her young charge would have to go about dressed in gold silk for the rest of the Season when Letitia burst into the shop.

'We must go, quickly,' she said in an urgent whisper.

Matilda stayed where she was, sitting in a tall chair by the counter. 'My dear girl, you have just purchased enough gold silk to cover most of Mayfair, and I would like an explanation.'

Letitia bent down and said in a low voice, 'I saw Clarisse. I followed her to an apothecary's. She bought arsenic.'

Matilda rose quickly. She handed the mercer her card. 'Have the silks sent to my address,' she said.

Both of them hurried out of the shop. Matilda told her coachman the address of Mrs Trumpington and ordered him to 'spring 'em.' But the coachman looked at the press of traffic ahead of him down Ludgate Hill and right along Fleet Street and said pessimistically that if they were able to move at all, it would be a miracle.

They crept over the now-filled-in dirty ditch called the Fleet River, along Fleet Street past the newspaper offices, the bookshops, the silversmiths, then along the Strand, past banks and taverns and bookshops, and so to Charing Cross where two miserable wretches in the stocks were being pelted with rotten vegetables and worse. Along Pall Mall, up St James's Street, past the clubs, across Piccadilly, and so to Mrs Trumpington's.

The butler opened the door and then reeled back as Letitia roughly pushed past him, dragging Matilda behind her. They ran up the stairs and burst into Mrs Trumpington's bedchamber.

She was sitting up in bed. There was a tray on her lap and Clarisse had just taken a spoonful of soup from a bowl on that tray and was holding it to the old lady's lips.

'NO!' cried Letitia. She hurtled forward and dashed the spoon from Mrs Trumpington's lips and then hurled tray, soup and all across the room.

Mrs Trumpington lay there, goggling.

'What are you doing?' demanded Clarisse. 'Madam is unwell.'

Letitia took a deep breath. 'Sir Charles suggested to you that Clarisse taste your food before you ate it, Mrs Trumpington. Did she taste that soup?'

'No. There is no need. Clarisse has been dismissed and I am changing my will this afternoon,' exclaimed Mrs Trumpington.

'Oh, Mrs Trumpington.' Letitia sighed. 'There was every need. If you died before this afternoon, would not Clarisse have inherited all?'

'I swear before God I am innocent,' said Clarisse, backing toward the door.

'Then why did you buy arsenic this morning?'

'Because . . . because, as I told madam, I use it for cosmetic purposes.'

Letitia's eyes narrowed. Clarisse was wearing a fine cambric apron with dainty pockets edged with lace.

'Turn out your pockets,' ordered Letitia.

Clarissa made a sudden dart for the door. Letitia was quicker. She seized the maid and lifted her up as easily as if she were a doll and placed her in the centre of the room. Then, holding her prisoner with one hand, she rummaged in her apron pockets with the other. 'Aha!' Letitia held up a small box with the apothecary's label on it. She released Clarisse and opened it. 'I notice a quantity of it has already been used.'

'I will not stay here any longer,' cried Clarisse. Letitia put up a hand to stop her but the maid darted under her arm and out.

'Catch her!' shouted Matilda. 'We will never know if we do not catch her.'

Letitia ran down the stairs with Matilda at her heels. They heard the street door slam. When they gained the pavement and looked desperately from left to right, there was no sign of the maid. Matilda went back indoors and explained to the horrified butler that Clarisse had without doubt tried to murder her mistress. The menservants were all sent out to search up and down the street, in the basements, in the shops, in the lanes and alleyways, but of the lady's maid there was no sign.

Clarisse was crouched in a cupboard under the stairs. She had dived for cover after banging the street door to make it sound as if she had fled outside. She waited, trying to control her ragged breathing, listening to the sounds of the hunt.

At last the searchers gave up. Matilda and Letitia stood in the hall. 'Now we will never know whether she killed the Countess of Torridon,' said Matilda.

'But we could prove she tried to murder Mrs

Trumpington,' said Letitia eagerly, 'and then perhaps if she were found guilty of that, she might confess to the other.'

'All she has to do is stick to her story that she takes a little arsenic to clear her skin,' said Matilda wearily. 'It is not uncommon.'

'But the soup! The remains of the soup!' cried Letitia. 'If traces of arsenic could be found in that . . .'

They went back upstairs to Mrs Trumpington's bedchamber. Letitia groaned aloud. Two chambermaids had just finished scrubbing the soiled carpet. Bowl, spoon and tray, one of them said in answer to Matilda's query, had been taken down to the kitchens and washed.

'Has she gone?' demanded Mrs Trumpington.

'Yes,' said Matilda, sinking down in a chair.

'Then we had better inform the authorities.'

Matilda put a hand to her brow. 'It would only mean more scandal. It would open up the whole nasty business again. And they may never find her, so all we would be left with would be speculation and gossip.'

Clarisse waited and waited. She was cramped and stiff and frightened, and yet the thought of those pretty clothes and jewels gave her strength. She could not get another position. In fact, she would have to go into hiding. In order to live, she would need to sell some of the finest jewels, those she had stolen from the Countess of Torridon. Rage against the dowager duchess boiled up in her. Clarisse loved each gown and trinket and jewel as a mother loves her children. At last she heard the butler make his nightly rounds, closing the shutters and bolting and locking the door. She waited for another hour until the house was absolutely quiet. Then she crept out, stifling a cry of pain that rose to her lips as she tried to straighten up. She crawled up the staircase, hanging onto the banister. Once in her room, she packed everything neatly and then carried each trunk down to the hall. Her heart in her mouth, she slid back the bolts and opened the door to the street and then carried each trunk out onto the pavement. Then she stood there, waiting for a hack, expecting any moment to hear a cry behind her. And then a hack came slowly down the street and dropped a gentleman at a house two doors away.

The jehu told Clarisse in a surly voice that he was going home and did not want another fare so she offered him a sovereign to take her to cheap lodgings anywhere outside the West End.

He agreed, although grumbling at the weight of Clarisse's trunks as he put them on the roof.

Then the hack moved off into the night. Clarisse was still nervous and on edge. She had very little actual cash. She would go to Ludgate Hill in the morning and pawn one of the countess's pieces of jewellery at Rundell & Bridge. It would be safer, admittedly, to go to some backstreet jeweller who would ask no questions, but would give her half the value. And one brooch should be able to keep her for some time to come.

EIGHT

The earl of Torridon had, with a great effort, stayed away from Matilda. She must be allowed time to make up her mind. But then he began to wonder if his absence might harden her resolve not to get married. He decided to buy her a present and take it along and then see if he could sweep aside any objections.

He made his way to the famous jeweller's, Rundell & Bridge, on Ludgate Hill. He stood looking in the windows at the glittering display. It would need to be something not too gaudy. His eye fell on a delicate little brooch made of fine diamonds and sapphires. That would be perfect. Then he frowned and took out his quizzing glass. There was something familiar about that brooch. He had a sudden feeling of *déjà vu*. When he had been courting his late wife and fancied himself in love, he had stood before this jeweller's window, just as he was standing now, looking at that self-same brooch.

He opened the shop door and went into the dark interior. The jeweller came forward and bowed low.

'That brooch,' said the earl. 'The one in the window of sapphires and diamonds. How did you come by it?'

'Only this morning, my lord,' said the jeweller. 'Of course I recognized it. We made it ourselves and you bought it quite some years ago. I suppose it has been through various hands since then.'

'Not to my knowledge,' said the earl grimly. 'Who brought it in?'

'Wait but a moment and I shall check our ledger. Here we are. A Mrs Jackson.'

'Address?'

'Forty-two Cheapside.'

'And what did this Mrs Jackson look like?'

'My lord, I trust nothing is wrong. She was a most genteel lady fallen on hard times. She was sallow of skin, black-eyed, slim, very finely gowned and soft spoken.'

Can it be Clarisse? thought the earl.

'I am sorry to tell you,' he said aloud, 'that the last time I saw that brooch it was in the possession of my late wife. Withdraw it from sale until I make some inquiries.'

'Of course, my lord. This is a most respectable firm. I would not have bought it had I thought there was anything suspect about the lady.'

The earl drove up and along Cheapside and reined

in his carriage outside number forty-two, which was a haberdasher's. He entered the shop to learn they had never heard of a Mrs Jackson, that the haberdasher and his family lived above the shop and did not take in lodgers.

He went back to St James's Square and told his butler to find her ladyship's jewel book. The room in which his wife had died had been locked up ever since her death and the earl had done nothing with her possessions. They had made joint wills shortly after their marriage, leaving everything to each other.

After a short time, the butler returned with a squat black book.

The earl opened it and began to scan the pages. 'Bring her jewel box as well,' he said.

Soon all the pieces were spread out on his desk and he examined and ticked off each one. All the items appeared to be accounted for in Clarisse's neat italic handwriting. He leaned back in his chair, the book in his hand. The ink and handwriting were peculiarly uniform, as if the whole book had been written in one go. He went through the items again, searching his memory. The brooch was missing. Then he remembered giving her another brooch with her initials in emeralds on a gold setting. That was gone.

The reason for Clarisse wishing to kill her mistress was becoming plain. And while Lady Torridon needed Clarisse to help in the pretence of pregnancy, then Clarisse would have a hold over the countess. But the night of the ball, that hold had been broken.

The earl had always been amazed at his wife's generosity toward the maid. He remembered one gown in particular of which the countess had been extremely fond, and yet she had given it to Clarisse.

He went out again, this time to Mrs Trumpington's, and listened, appalled, to the old lady's tale of attempted murder. 'And she must have been hiding in the house, the cunning vixen,' said Mrs Trumpington, 'for in the morning all her things had gone.'

'And you did not report her to the authorities?'

'I would have done, but the duchess pointed out there was no real proof and all that would happen would be a lot of nasty scandal.'

'I have just discovered she thieved some of my wife's jewels and so I will report her now. Good heavens, do you not see? If she is not arrested for something, she may murder someone else, for I am now convinced it was she who poisoned my wife.'

The earl went to the magistrate in Bow Street and laid charges of theft against Clarisse Perdaux, 'although,' he added, 'I am now convinced that is an assumed name, for I am sure she is not French, but it is the name she has been using for some time. In Rundell & Bridge, she used the name Jackson.'

He offered a reward of a thousand guineas, and then made his way to Matilda's while wanted posters were rapidly printed and posted all over London, the ink still wet from the printer's.

When he entered Matilda's drawing room, he found not only Matilda but Sir Charles and Letitia. He briefly told them what he had discovered and Sir

Charles clapped his small hands in delight. 'Now we have her!' he said.

'But we need proof that she killed the Countess of Torridon,' said Matilda wearily. 'After all this time, the evidence will be only circumstantial.'

'With all these wanted posters going up in London,' said Sir Charles slowly, 'she will find it impossible to sell anything else. She cannot work. Sooner or later, she will have to come out of hiding.'

'Sir Charles,' said the earl, 'can you not take Miss Plumtree for a walk in the Park? I wish to be alone with the duchess.'

Matilda turned quite pale but said in a low voice, 'Do leave us.'

Letitia went to fetch her bonnet. Sir Charles was turning over in his mind ways in which he might be able to find the missing Clarisse.

When Letitia and Sir Charles had gone out, the earl sat on the sofa next to Matilda and took her hand in his. 'I have stayed away from you,' he said, 'to give you time to make up your mind.'

Matilda looked at him sadly. 'You must understand, Torridon, that I dread the scandal. I loathe all this murder business, all this dark crime. I have not recovered from my husband's death. I still see him lying there with his life blood spilling out.' She shuddered.

'So you will not marry me?'

'Give me a little more time,' pleaded Matilda.

'I see what it is,' he said bitterly. 'Your passion cannot equal mine or you would marry me tomorrow and let the tattletales of this world rot in hell. I could *shake* you.'

'Do not bully me,' said Matilda. 'I have had enough of murder and mayhem to last me a lifetime!'

'Then it must be a lifetime without me.' The earl strode from the room and Matilda burst into tears.

Emma and Annabelle, who were just arriving, nearly collided with the enraged earl. They went upstairs to find Matilda in floods of tears.

'The brute,' cried Emma. 'Has he not done enough damage? You must tell your servants to forbid him in the house!'

Matilda dried her eyes. 'I am a disgrace,' she said. 'I am so very weak. He despises me.'

'Who is that Scotch oaf to despise such as you?' said Annabelle hotly.

'I had better tell you all, my dear friends,' said Matilda wearily. 'The Countess of Torridon's lady's maid, Clarisse, took up employ with our old friend Mrs Trumpington. Mrs Trumpington was much taken with her, so much so that she planned to leave everything in her will to Clarisse. My charge, Letitia, is being courted by Sir Charles Follett. He suspected that Mrs Trumpington, who was ill, was suffering from arsenical poisoning. He had all arsenic removed from the house and convinced the old lady to change her will. Yesterday morning on Ludgate Hill while I was in the mercers' with Letitia, she saw Clarisse going past and ran out and followed her. The maid bought arsenic in Creed Lane. We got to Mrs Trumpington's in time to stop her drinking soup that

I am now convinced was laced with arsenic. Clarisse escaped us. The earl has just discovered that she has sold a brooch belonging to his late wife. We did not know before what the maid's motive for killing the countess could possibly be. There is a warrant out for her arrest for theft but, after all this time, it will be nigh impossible to prove she murdered the countess.'

'And is that why you are crying?' asked Emma.

'I am crying because the earl has obtained a special licence and wishes me to marry him and I cannot while there is all this murder and mystery and scandal.'

'Matilda,' said Annabelle, 'you were bullied dreadfully by the duke. You cannot possibly be contemplating marriage to a man who will bully you as well.'

'I love him,' said Matilda flatly. 'I am wretched without him.'

Annabelle shook her head in amazement. 'Can this be our Matilda? The bold and resolute Matilda. Why, if those are your feelings, you must forget about scandal and nonsense and marry him! If *he* was suspected of his wife's murder, I could see your point.'

'He will not want to marry me now,' said Matilda, large tears rolling down her face. 'I am so silly. I have led such an irregular sort of life, I wanted safety, security, tenderness, not this burning passion.'

'There now,' said Emma. 'If he loves you very much, he will wait, and if you love him very much, you will send for him.'

'But love is supposed to be happy, tender! Not burning and aching as if one had the fever.'

The two matrons exchanged smiles across Matilda's bent head.

'I would marry him, Matilda. Frustration is all that is up with you,' said Emma, and then laughed. 'We must sound as bold and brazen as American women at the dinner table.' In America, the ladies always dined separately from the men and tales of the alarming frankness of their speech when they were in their cups startled many visiting Englishwomen.

'But there is Letitia,' pointed out Matilda. 'It would be cruel to pack her off home so quickly.'

'As to that,' said Emma, 'she can stay with me for the rest of the Season. She will probably marry Sir Charles. They are the talk of London.'

'Letitia even survived a visit to Sir Charles's dreadful mother,' said Matilda. 'But he is about the first man she met. I would like to see her having a chance to meet others.'

'Worry about yourself. Send your earl a note telling him you will marry him and that will be an end of it.'

'Give me a few days to think,' pleaded Matilda.

'It has nothing to do with us,' pointed out Emma. 'But do not leave him too long or he may propose to someone else out of sheer bad temper!'

Letitia and Sir Charles walked slowly through the Park. 'Where in the whole of this metropolis would Clarisse go?' asked Sir Charles.

'I do not know,' said Letitia. 'I would not know where to begin to look. She may have left the country.'

'Soon she will need money.' Sir Charles stood stock still. 'I have the glimmerings of an idea. But first we have to find her.'

'She will see the wanted posters and change her appearance. She could now look quite different.'

'I was very good at amateur theatricals,' said Sir Charles. 'It is amazing – the best way to change one's appearance is to do something very simple but people always go too far. I would wager anything that Clarisse had dyed her hair red, altered her shape with cushions, and put wax pads in her cheeks to change the shape of her face.'

'Oh, wonderful,' said Letitia. 'All we have to do is search among the thousands of people in London for a fat woman with red hair.'

'Let me think. You saw her in Ludgate Hill, did you not? And the earl said she gave an address in Cheapside. So she is probably hiding somewhere in the City.'

'Thousands in the City,' said Letitia gloomily.

'But not late at night. And late at night is when she will probably emerge to buy food.'

'How can we patrol the City streets at night? Matilda would never let me out. We are to go to the opera tonight, and I must admit I am looking forward to it. I have never been to the opera before.'

'I shall take you to hundreds of operas,' said Sir Charles. 'Could you not plead the headache and slip out of the house, say, at about midnight? I could be waiting with my carriage at the corner of the street.'

'Very well.' Letitia began to laugh. 'We are quite mad, you know. A lady as tall as myself and a gentleman as finely dressed as you will attract a lot of attention.'

He frowned and then his face cleared. 'I could purchase a suit of men's clothes for you and we will both be plainly dressed, like a couple of shopkeepers. Is there a servant who would take the clothes for you and not say anything?'

'There is the duchess's page, Peter. He is devoted to her and would do anything if he thought he was helping her.'

'Then take him into your confidence and send him to my lodgings at six. I will give him the clothes.'

'How will you be able to choose a suit of clothes to fit me?'

Sir Charles flushed slightly. He had gone over every inch of her body in his imagination. 'Do not worry,' he said. 'They will fit.'

Letitia was relieved when she returned to find that Matilda had gone to lie down and had left word she would not be well enough to go to the opera that evening. Summoned to Letitia's bedchamber, the page, Peter, listened open-mouthed as Letitia told him the story of the murdering lady's maid. 'You see, Peter,' said Letitia, 'if you aid me in this deception, you will be helping your mistress. For she will break her heart if she does not marry Torridon, and yet she is afraid to marry him until the death of his wife is explained.'

'Can I come with you?' begged Peter. 'I can see in the dark excellent well.'

'But you do not know what Clarisse looks like.'

'I remember her well. I was lamp boy at Ramillies and went out walking to Hadsborough one day. The countess was driving through with a lady beside her and folks told me it was the countess and her lady's maid. I marked her particularly for she looked too haughty and grand to be a servant. I have a good memory for faces.'

'If Sir Charles does not object, you may come with us.'

Sir Charles would have liked to object strongly when he saw the page following Letitia along the street, for he had been looking forward to sharing the adventure with her and with her alone. But the boy looked so excited and happy that Sir Charles had not the heart to send him away. He complimented Letitia on her appearance, saying she made a very fine shopkeeper. Letitia was wearing a brown coat over a plain waistcoat, buff trousers, and Hessian boots. Her beaver hat felt tight for she had crammed her thick tresses up under it. Sir Charles, minus paint and jewels and finery, looked very strange to Letitia. She adored his normally elaborate clothes.

They drove to the City and along Cheapside. Sir Charles's groom held the horses, and then the three set off to patrol the streets of the City on foot.

* * *

Clarisse was very hungry and very frightened. She had seen that poster that afternoon offering a reward for her capture. She had promptly given up her lodgings and moved to new lodgings in Pudding Lane, talking in a broad country voice and introducing herself as a widow. The poster had fortunately described her as a French maid. Clarisse, as the earl and Sir Charles had rightly suspected, was not French. She was the daughter of a farm labourer from Kent, brought up, one of ten, in filth and poverty. She was bright and so the local schoolteacher had taken pity on her and taught her her letters and found her a post in a local household. From there, having obtained a good reference, Clarisse had travelled to London, again finding a post as a housemaid, but in a noble household. She envied the lady's maids of society, with their airs and their fine clothes. She was well aware of the vogue for French maids, and so, when she had obtained a post as a housemaid in the Countess of Torridon's household, she had set about making it look as if the countess's lady's maid was stealing things. When she exposed the 'guilty' maid to the countess, she had told her she was in fact French, and had only changed her name out of fear of English prejudice. The countess was delighted to have a French maid to replace the one she had just fired, and so Clarisse got the post.

She waited in the dingy little room that was now her home. There was not room enough to hang away all her gowns and they lay piled up on the bed, the rich stuff shimmering in the candlelight. Clarisse did not know what to do. Any jeweller, even one who consorted with criminals, would gladly turn her over for that reward.

She decided that if she had something to eat and drink, then she might hit upon a plan. She had one mourning gown. One of the countess's relatives had died a few years before and the countess, who had taken her maid to the funeral, had bought her a black gown and black straw hat with a heavy veil. Now Clarisse put them on. People, she knew, were apt to shy away from anyone in mourning.

It was four-thirty in the morning. Practically all the taverns and chop houses were closed. But there were a few, she knew, that would open soon down in Lower Thames Street to serve the porters of Billingsgate fish market.

She let herself quietly out of the building. Above her stood the Monument to the Great Fire of London, pointing up into the night sky. She scurried down Pudding Lane where the Great Fire had started and along Lower Thames Street and past the grim walls of St Dunstan's workhouse. A great clanging bell sounded, a signal that the market was opening for business. The sky was lightening by the minute but Clarisse was so very hungry, she was determined, despite the risk, to find something to eat.

'This is ridiculous,' said Letitia, and then gave a cavernous yawn. 'We have walked miles and miles and looked and looked.'

They had just left Smithfield Market. 'I was sure it

would be one of the markets,' mourned Sir Charles. 'We have tried Leadenhall.'

'There's Billingsgate,' volunteered Peter.

Letitia groaned.

'Billingsgate it is. But this time we'll take my carriage,' said Sir Charles. 'We can always leave it close by. Just let us try Billingsgate. I wish I had brought some wax for your ears, Miss Plumtree, for the porters of Billingsgate and the fishwives are foul-mouthed beyond belief.'

They walked back to Cheapside where the groom was walking the horses up and down. It was a relief to Letitia to sink into the upholstered seat of Sir Charles's well-sprung carriage. Her eyelids began to droop. She had long ago decided they would never find Clarisse and had only stayed in the hunt to enjoy as much of Sir Charles's company as she could.

They left the carriage in Lower Thames Street, some distance from the market. Letitia had to be shaken awake. Sir Charles was showing no signs of fatigue and neither was Peter. He was like a small dog on the hunt, thought Letitia. Not for one moment had he looked less than excited and alert. 'Places here all right,' murmured Sir Charles as they approached the market. Stalls of all kinds. And a pie shop, all open and doing a brisk business.

'Look!' said Peter. 'There's a lady sitting at a table by the window.'

'I can see nothing but a black smeary blur,' said Sir Charles crossly. 'Poor glass.'

'Let me go in,' pleaded Peter. 'She might recognize you.'

'Dear boy,' murmured Sir Charles as Peter disappeared into the shop. 'Such enthusiasm. He sees her everywhere. Do you remember that old crone at Smithfield? I had to forcibly restrain him from challenging her.'

Peter came back out, his eyes gleaming in the light from the pie shop windows. 'It could be her,' he said. 'She's all in black, like mourning, and she's got a heavy veil over her face. She isn't a fishwife or a costermonger so what's she doing in a pie shop at this hour of the morning? If only she would raise that veil.'

'If she wants to eat, she'll need to raise her veil,' said Sir Charles in a bored voice. Peter darted back into the shop again. 'Bless the boy,' exclaimed Sir Charles. 'The fatiguing enthusiasm of youth! You are like a beautiful horse, my love. I swear you are about to sleep standing up.'

Peter came out again. 'It's her,' he said, dancing about them on the pavement. 'Shall I call the constable?'

'It can't be. It's impossible.' Letitia stared at him in amazement.

'You had better let me look,' said Sir Charles. 'Your height makes you conspicuous, Miss Plumtree.' He pulled his broad-brimmed hat down over his eyes and sauntered into the shop. He bought a meat pie and waited while it was wrapped in newspaper, his eyes ranging round the small room with its few tables. Most of the customers were costermongers, buying pies to take out and eat at the stalls in the market. He saw the black-clad figure of a woman. She was eating greedily, holding the pie with both hands, crouched over the table. It was indeed Clarisse.

He took the pie he had bought outside and said urgently, 'It is she. Good work, Peter. Walk away a little. We must follow her and find out where she's holed up.'

Peter, his voice quite squeaky with disappointment, said, 'But we could catch her now.'

'I have other plans,' said Sir Charles. 'You, Peter, must be the one to follow her, for the three of us would look too noticeable.'

They waited in the shadows until they saw her emerge. She was now heavily veiled. Peter slipped away and followed her. Letitia and Sir Charles waited anxiously.

'But what is your plan?' asked Letitia. 'It is a miracle we found her. Why not call the watch or the constable or anyone? She will escape us again.'

'I cannot tell you my plan,' said Sir Charles. 'Even now it strikes me as insane. You would only protest. But do one thing for me. Tell that dowager duchess to marry the earl as soon as possible, for if my plan works and I get a confession to the murder of Lady Torridon out of Clarisse, the earl will think the duchess's love is too weak to take him unless things are respectable. He might reject her out of pique.'

'I will do all I can,' promised Letitia. 'That is if I can manage to stay awake this day. I hope that boy comes to no harm. What if she should kill him?'

'Arsenic is her game and she's hardly likely to stuff it down his throat in the middle of a London street. Have some pie?'

Letitia shuddered and waved it away. 'After all this talk of arsenic, I could not eat a thing.'

They waited anxiously while the sun came up, burning red through the forest of masts on the river.

Then they heard a light patter of feet and Peter came running toward them.

'Pudding Lane,' he said. 'Number twenty-seven. *Now* can we take her?'

'Sir Charles has some mysterious plan, Peter,' said Letitia. 'I have decided to trust him and I think you should, too.'

Sir Charles looked at the boy's downcast face. 'Have you not had enough of adventure for one night, boy?'

'I could never have enough adventure,' said Peter. 'I would be a soldier if my mistress were happily settled.'

'She soon will be,' said Sir Charles. 'I shall reward you for this night's work, my boy. If we pull it off, I shall buy you your colours in a good regiment.'

Overcome, Peter began to cry with gratitude. Letitia stooped and kissed Sir Charles on the cheek. 'You are the best of men.'

'I wish that boy were in Jericho right now,'

muttered Sir Charles, who longed to take Letitia in his arms.

He almost changed his mind and decided not to help Peter's future career in the army, for the boy stuck close to them, munching the pie Sir Charles had bought at Billingsgate, right to Bolton Street, and so he was forced to limit himself to a modest kiss on Letitia's hand.

Letitia opened one eye and looked at the clock. Two in the afternoon! She struggled from bed and dressed with speed, then hurtled down the stairs and crashed into the drawing room. Matilda looked up in surprise. 'What is the matter, dear?'

'You,' garbled Letitia. 'You must marry Lord Torridon. You must tell him as soon as possible that you will marry him.'

'I do not want to hurt you,' said Matilda stiffly. 'But I fear you are being impertinent.'

Letitia seized her by the shoulders and shook her hard. 'You silly woman!' she shouted, and then sat down and burst into tears.

'No, don't cry,' said Matilda. 'I am not angry with you.' She patted Letitia helplessly on the shoulder. That remark of Letitia's, that 'silly woman', had shaken Matilda to the core. For that is what she now seemed in her own eyes, a rabbit of a woman, so afraid of the gossips that she was prepared to throw away the earl's love. 'Do not feel so strongly on my behalf, Letitia. You are overwrought. The servants could not wake you. Are you ill?'

Letitia dried her eyes and blew her nose and said, 'I am tired. I have been walking the streets of the City all night long. We found Clarisse.'

She then told the amazed Matilda all about her adventures, finishing up with the desperate plea, 'So do you not see now why you must tell the earl you will marry him? For Sir Charles says if he gains this confession and then you tell the earl, he will think your love for him is so shallow that you needs must wait until all is respectable. And I must say candidly that it would look to me very like that if I were in Torridon's shoes.'

Letitia waited impatiently while Matilda lectured her on the folly of dressing in men's clothes and going out all night with Sir Charles and unchaperoned. Letitia had not mentioned Peter, not wanting to get the boy into trouble. 'For,' said Matilda severely, 'if it ever got about, he would have to marry you.'

'Do not tempt me,' muttered Letitia, but Matilda was now too worried to hear her. Would the earl come if she sent for him? Or would he be too furious with her? Goodness! He may even have decided to go back to Scotland.

Sir Charles strolled into the offices of the *Morning Recorder* in Fleet Street and asked for Mr Hughes. He knew Mr Hughes of old. Did not all society? Hughes was always sniffing about and had an uncanny nose for scandal. The reporter was sitting at a grubby desk, wearing a pair of ink-stained linen sleeves to protect his shirt.

'Sir Charles!' he said, backing a pace. Mr Hughes had had visits from the Quality before, usually gentlemen carrying horsewhips.

'Sit down, man, and listen,' said Sir Charles. 'I am going to give you the story of a lifetime and lead you to catch a murderess.'

After Sir Charles had left, Mr Hughes carefully removed his sleeves and put on his coat and hat. He wondered whether to talk to his editor or not, but decided against it. Tricks had been played on him before by young sprigs of the nobility, and he did not want to look a fool. But if this was a trick, it was an expensive one, for Sir Charles had just given him five thousand golden guineas.

He walked briskly along Fleet Street, up Ludgate Hill, past St Paul's and along Cheapside, and then to the Monument and down Pudding Lane. He stopped outside number twenty-seven. It was an old clothes shop with rooms above.

He pushed his way into the musty shop. The owner looked as ragged and smelly as his stock.

'Got any rooms?' asked Mr Hughes, jerking his head at the ceiling.

'Only one and that's been taken by a widder.'

'Know everyone in the City. What's her name?'

'Widder Brown.'

'My stars! Not the widow Brown. Known her since I was this high. I'll pop up and pay her a call. Get through the back of the shop, do I?'

'No, entrance in the alley atter back.'

Mr Hughes walked along until he found a smelly

close leading to an alley along the back off the shops. He counted his way along until he reached the back of the old clothes shop. There was a rickety stair leading up to the first floor. He took a deep breath and mounted, then hammered on the door.

There was a long silence and then a female voice demanded, 'Who is it?'

'Come fer the rent,' said Mr Hughes, imitating the old clothes seller's voice to the best of his ability.

'I paid you a month in advance.'

'That ain't what it says in my here book,' whined Mr Hughes.

The door jerked open. Clarisse saw him and tried to close it. Mr Hughes thrust his foot in the door and then put his shoulder to it, forcing the door open and, at the same time, pushing her back into the room.

'Who are you?' Clarisse was white to the lips.

'A friend,' said Mr Hughes. He pulled forward a chair and sat down on it, leaning his back against the door. 'I am come to help you.'

'How? Why?' demanded Clarisse, her eyes darting this way and that as if seeking escape.

He held up the heavy wash leather bag full of guineas. 'Name of Hughes,' he said laconically. 'Journalist with the *Morning Recorder*. Pay you five thou' for your story.'

Clarisse gave a bitter laugh. 'And then send me to the hangman?'

'No, I'll play fair. You write down how and why you killed the Countess of Torridon and I'll get you to the stage leaving for the coast and give you the money. When I consider you are safely out of the country, I'll publish it.'

'I will do no such thing. I am innocent.'

'Oh, well.' Mr Hughes sighed. 'I'll just turn you over. You'll hang anyway, or, if you're lucky, you'll get burned on the hand and transported for a thief. If you take my advice, hanging's a better death. Quicker. Better than rotting out your life on a leaky ship bound for the colonies. You won't have any of those pretty gowns left, I tell you.'

Clarisse looked frantically at her gowns spread out on the bed and back to Mr Hughes. 'How can I trust you?'

'You can't,' said Mr Hughes cheerfully. 'But for what it's worth, you have my word. That story's worth a fortune to me.'

'Take a glass of wine with me,' said Clarisse.

Mr Hughes grinned. 'No, I thank you. I have a desire to live. Go on. Look in the bag. Gold guineas. Enough to keep you on the continent till you die.'

'What do you want me to do?' asked Clarisse after looking in the bag.

'You tell me how you topped Torridon's missus, I give you the money and put you on the stagecoach. We'll look like a couple. Get you to the booking office and then it's up to you to make sure one of the passengers doesn't recognize you.'

'And you will not trick me?'

Mr Hughes solemnly crossed his heart.

Clarisse sat down suddenly in a battered armchair as if all the strength had gone out of her legs.

'Very well,' she said in a tired voice. Mr Hughes masked his elation, took out a lead pencil and a note-book, licked the end of the pencil, and began to write as, in a flat emotionless voice, Clarisse described how she had poisoned the Countess of Torridon.

For half an hour she talked, not only of the killing, but of her early life and how she had come to London and how she had pretended to be French . . . Her real name was Jackson, she said.

When it was over, Mr Hughes got her to sign the confession, solemnly handed her the bag of guineas, and tucked his notebook away in one of his capacious pockets.

'Now, then,' said Mr Hughes cheerfully, 'I'll take you to the stage and see you on your way.'

Clarisse sat there looking white and drained.

'I say, bustle about,' said Mr Hughes anxiously. 'Time's passing.'

'Await me below,' said Clarisse. 'As you can see I am in my undress and I need to pack.'

'No funny business,' warned Mr Hughes.

Clarisse gave him a tired smile. 'You need not fear. You have my confession. I must trust you. Wait outside at the foot of the stairs. There is no other way out.'

Mr Hughes went down the stairs and leaned on the rickety post at the foot. He felt quite dizzy with elation. Now all he needed to do was put her on the stage and then go to Bow Street and tell the runners to pick her up at the first stop. He had promised Sir Charles his money would be retrieved and returned to him. He basked in the glory to come. Then after some time, he glanced at his watch. She was taking a very long time. What if she had escaped him? He could not dare publish that confession. He would be arrested himself for having let her escape the gallows.

He darted up the stairs and hammered at the door. 'Come along,' he called. Nothing. Silence.

He began to panic. What if there was another way out of that room? Fear lent him strength. He ran at the door and crashed it down off its hinges.

She was lying on the bed, dressed in a beautiful morning gown, with jewels sparkling at her ears and at her breast. Her face was dreadfully contorted. On the floor lay a glass and, beside the glass, an apothecary's box, half full of white powder.

Poisoned herself, thought Mr Hughes with relief. I can say I found her dead and the confession was lying beside her. Demme, no. They'll take it away. I'll say she posted it to me. That's it.

Her jewels were lying around the room. A thin necklace of diamonds and pearls caught his eye. He knew just the little lady who would appreciate such a trinket. Danced every night at the Coal Hole in The Strand. He put it in his pocket, picked up the bag of guineas, and went off whistling to tell the authorities Clarisse had been found.

The earl arrived after receiving a note from Matilda begging him to come.

He dared not hope she had come to her senses. He dreaded her telling him to go away forever.

When he entered the drawing room, Letitia rose quickly, curtsied to him and walked out. She closed the door firmly behind her and then pressed her ear to the panels.

Matilda rose to her feet and held out both hands, smiling at the earl shyly. He drew her against him and smiled down at her with relief, seeing her answer in her eyes. He kissed her eyes and then her neck and then her mouth, and she wound her fingers in his black hair and strained against him. They sank down onto the sofa and he lay on top of her, crushing her mouth with his, his hands ranging over her fevered body. All their pent-up passion was driving them both mad. They had not said a word. She did not even pro--test when he broke the tapes of her gown and pulled it down to bare her breasts and then ripped open his own shirt, sending the buttons flying, so that he could feel her breasts against his naked chest.

Letitia listened outside the door in an agony of worry. Matilda was supposed to tell him she loved him, not sit there in a sulky silence.

At last Letitia could bear it no longer. I am going to give them both a piece of my mind, she thought.

She opened the door and walked in. She stood dismayed. The room appeared to be empty. Then she heard a rustling sound coming from the sofa and walked across the room and peered over the high back.

Letitia's face flamed scarlet. She inched her way backward until she reached the door and then closed it with trembling fingers.

She turned and found herself looking down at Sir Charles. He looked up at her blushing face and then back at the closed door of the drawing room. He took her hand and led her downstairs. When they had reached the hall, he said sympathetically, 'Am I right in guessing they got together at last?'

Letitia nodded dumbly.

'I say, is there anywhere we might be alone?' asked Sir Charles.

'There's the library,' said Letitia. 'No one uses it much. It's such a dreary room.'

'It'll do. Lead me to it.'

Letitia opened the door and they walked inside. She turned to face him. 'You have news for me?'

'It is the most wonderful news.' He told her about approaching the reporter. 'Clarisse gave Hughes of the *Morning Recorder* her signed confession before taking arsenic herself.'

'She has confessed to the murder of the Countess of Torridon?'

'Right down to the amount of poison, why she did it, and where she put it. Seems she was blackmailing the countess over the deception and when the earl found out his wife was not pregnant, the countess told Clarisse to hand back all the gowns and jewels and take herself off to the streets.'

'But why poison her?' exclaimed Letitia. 'Even cast off without a reference, she could have found something, and surely she could have sold the gowns and jewellery to keep her for some time.'

'It was the idea of handing them back,' said Sir

Charles. 'Told Hughes she couldn't bear to part with even a shred of cloth. Said when she sold that brooch to Rundell & Bridge, she cried the whole way home. Mad. Quite mad.'

Letitia clasped her hands. 'But this is wonderful, Sir Charles. We must go and tell them immediately.' She blushed rosy red as she remembered what the couple upstairs were doing.

'Forget about them,' said Sir Charles. 'It's always them.' He saw a footstool in the corner, fetched it, and carried it toward her.

The library door opened and Peter stood there. 'I heard you were come, sir,' he said. 'I wondered if there was any news.'

Sir Charles threw down the footstool. 'Is there no privacy in this house?' he cried.

Letitia put a hand on his shoulder. 'Peter deserves to hear how clever you have been, Sir Charles. After all, it was Peter who found her.'

He sighed and then patiently told Peter all about how Clarisse had been tricked into making the confession.

'She cannot have trusted Hughes,' said Peter.

'No, Hughes thinks that after she had told him all, she realized that even if he did not betray her, it was more than likely she would be caught before she could get a ship to take her across the Channel.

'Sometimes one has to wait two weeks before a boat can sail. Or perhaps, after telling him everything, the full enormity of what she had done struck her. We will never know.'

'Never know what?' said the earl's voice from the doorway. Matilda was standing beside him, looking happy. Letitia noticed that Matilda's gown had been securely pinned at the breast and blushed, remembering that scene in the drawing room.

'Sir Charles has catched that murderess!' cried Peter, and so Sir Charles had to tell his story again when all he wanted was to be alone with Letitia.

'This calls for a celebration,' said Matilda. 'Come upstairs to the drawing room, Sir Charles. We shall drink to your success, and,' she said, taking the earl's hand in her own, 'to my future marriage.'

Letitia hugged Matilda, wished her well and kissed the earl on the cheek. Then as the earl and Matilda were leaving the room with Peter behind them, Sir Charles saw Letitia was about to follow them. He pulled her back and closed the door.

'Stay right there,' he ordered. He placed the footstool firmly in front of her and climbed up on it.

He put his hands on her shoulders and looked anxiously into her warm brown eyes. And the normally elegant and mannered Sir Charles Follett blurted out like a schoolboy, 'Can I marry you?'

Oh, how she smiled and how her eyes glowed and how she laughed before she said, 'I thought you would never ask me.'

He took her face in his hands and kissed her gently on the lips. It was like kissing summer, he thought in an incoherent way, warmth, and sunshine and fields of flowers.

Letitia swayed in his arms, hearing all the church

bells of London crashing a wedding peal in her ears.

When she could speak, she said softly, 'Would you mind very much if my wedding gown were of gold silk?'

'I would not mind if you were married in rags,' he said fervently. 'But why?'

'Because . . . because . . . oh, Charles. Kiss me again!'